THROUGH MARIA'S EYES

By

Linda Sunshine
and David Rich

Through Maria's Eyes
A novelization of the screenplay by Scott Walker

Copyright © 2010 by DB Rich Productions, LLC

Published by DB Rich Productions, LLC

ISBN: 978-0-578-06880-0

Front Cover Designed by Joe Holt, Scott Walker and David Rich
Front Photo Credit by Flickr-A6U571N
Rear Cover Designed by David Rich
Rear Photo Design by Joe Holt

Printed in the United States of America

For My Mom,

A Promise Kept

PROLOGUE

Lights Danced
on the Danube

⁓✵⁓

People always ask: Why didn't you leave?

I am almost 92 years old now and all this happened a very long time ago but still, even today, the same question: Why didn't you get out?

The question comes from strangers and from the people closest to me—my children and grandchildren, this beautiful American family my husband and I created in order to go on living. They are my heart and soul but, then, so was my other family, the flesh and bones and mostly ashes I left behind when we finally emigrated from the displaced persons camp in Germany in the late 1940s.

Why didn't your family get out sooner? They all want to know but I do not know how to answer.

I am haunted by all the unanswered questions. There is no

place for 'why' in my life. There is only what happened and what I know to be true.

For years, I tried so hard to forget. I wanted to start life over, to begin anew, to bury the past beneath the rubble that was Central Europe after the Allies rescued us. But I discovered that forgetting is an illusion. If the memories don't materialize during the day, they come during the long dark nights when emotions and feelings take hold over the body and cling with the tenacity of barnacles on sharp coral reef. The memories cascade over me: the way it was to live the way we lived, with death and the fear of getting captured ever present—those dreadful and disturbing sense memories are never far away for very long.

In America, I had my two little boys to bring up so I tried to ignore the ghosts that haunted my dreams, the night terrors that left my body drenched with sweat. Often, I'd awake with an echo of a scream still ringing in my throat. My husband, Steven, would hold me until the fear drained away and my heart stopped racing. Then, as always, a cold determination would seep into my bones—I would stay alive, I would protect my loved ones, I would get us all to safety. That is the determination that replaced the young, innocent heart of my youth and made it possible for me to save the ones I could save. But every day I live with the ghosts of those I could not protect.

Survival was the only thing that mattered, despite anything we had to do or any pretense we used to live. Just survive until tomorrow, I would tell my sister Heidi. Keep breathing in and out; wait to see what the morning brings. This is what kept us alive all those months we were forced to live a secret life, to deny our family, our heritage and our God.

So many miracles kept us alive, so many moments when

fate intervened in our favor. Even then we could not believe how we managed to go on living. I don't care how many books you have read or how many movies you have seen, if you were not there you cannot imagine what it was like. Every day of life was a miracle.

My sister is long gone now—God rest her soul—like all the others. I am the only one left who lived through it, the only one who knows how much we endured and the strength it took to survive. And now, after all those American years of working so hard to forget, only now, at the end of my life, I am trying, once again, to remember it all.

I go back to the journal I wrote so many years ago. "Write it all down," Steven would say as he cradled me in his arms late at night. "Remembering will help you to forget." I was still a young woman then, not even forty-five. And so, to erase the dreams, I began to remember, a little bit every day. I recorded everything I could recall from that time in Hungary, from before the madness began.

Steven bought me a small tape recording machine and I spoke into it. During the 60s and 70s, my days were filled taking care of my children, my husband, our home and Steven's medical practice. I had little time to record my thoughts but, at night, when all I had were my thoughts, I spent hours recording on that tiny machine. One tape after another, night after night, my story spooled out before me.

I had tried to write it down in English, this strange language so unlike Hungarian or Yiddish that Steven and I worked hard to master. We studied English the whole time we were living in the displaced persons camp. We thought that if we learned the language we'd have a better chance at coming to the United States and starting life again as Americans. Oh, how we dreamed of America! But writing in English was challenging—it is such a difficult language, full of quirks and nuances—and once I got the machine, I could speak more easily in my own language.

Then, one day, after dozens of tapes, I was done talking. I had told my story; I was finished with it.

I wanted to burn the tapes, along with the memories but Steven said, "No, the memories are who we are. This is our past, our legacy to those who come after us. And the children will need it when they are older. The world must never forget what happened."

Steven found a translator who wrote down my words and typed them out in proper English. He put the pages into a hardcover binder. I remember the look and feel of those pale, almost translucent, onionskin pages. I held them and wept. The pages were all uniform and looked so, I don't know, *official* is the only word that comes to mind. Yes, all this really happened and I survived to tell the story.

So I did not burn the pages. I did what my husband wanted. I always did what he wanted because I loved him, because he was usually right about such things and because I was raised to believe that in a marriage the wife does what her husband says. (I know, my grandchildren would argue with me on this point but this is what I learned from my own dear mother.)

I wrapped the binder in a red silk scarf that had belonged to my sister Rose; it was all I had left of her. Then I buried the journal in a trunk in the attic, thinking I'd never look at it again.

The past was over and done for me on that day.

So now, when my memory is not so good anymore, thanks to Steven I have these pages to remind me what really happened and to tell my story to those who have come after me.

After reading it all again I still cannot explain why we stayed in Budapest, even after the government fell to the Nazis and the world became an impossibly dangerous place for Jews. I guess we stayed because we did not know how to leave and could not believe we really had to.

What happened in those last horrible months before liberation was beyond anything we could have anticipated.

How can you imagine the unimaginable, much less prepare for it?

We stayed because it was hard to leave; visas were more precious than diamonds and, besides, we had no place to go. Homeless, stateless Jews roamed all over Central Europe, and no one wanted them. Hungary was our home. My family had lived in and around Budapest for generations; it was the only life we knew. Leave? Where to?

My father felt he could not leave because he was a Rabbi, the spiritual leader of our congregation. Also, as the *Shochet*, trained to slaughter animals in the proper kosher tradition, my father was essential to the Jews living in Budapest, who could not keep kosher without him. A leader cannot abandon his people, he would tell us.

Mostly though, I think, we stayed because of our belief in *Bashert*, which you might translate to mean destiny or fate or maybe just "God's will." My father and mother believed there was a reason for everything. "God helps those who help themselves," my father would say. Like so many others, he trusted in the will of God to protect his people. You may ask, as so many do, where was God in that God-forsaken time and place? Why did he abandon all those millions of people?

I can only repeat that there is no place for "why" in my life. There is only *Bashert*.

Yes, I am almost 92 years old now, and I repeat things, I know I do. I can see the frustration in the faces of my children when I am speaking. They do not understand that my life plays in an endless loop in my head. I can remember the oddest things: street names in Budapest—Dohány, Magdolna, Kirayli Csanyi, that my children can't even pronounce, the color of a dress I wore to a tea party at the Hotel Gellert on a warm summer afternoon, the smell of my mother's cooking for Shabbat dinner and the music! Oh yes, the music! Those mournful, crying gypsy violins were everywhere in Budapest, on the streets and wafting out the windows of the ornate hotels that lined the glorious Danube. My beloved Budapest was so beautiful then.

At twilight, we walked along the banks of the river. The yellow light from the big street lamps danced off the water like stars twinkling in the sky. All along the riverbank were benches where sweethearts sat listening to those impossibly sad gypsy violins that played all night long. Whenever I hear a violin, I think of the Danube with the moon hanging yellow and gold over the water. At least that is the way I remember it, all glowing and calmly romantic.

We were so innocent. We did not know what was coming so we were happy with small things. Sitting on a public bench, enjoying the evening air, holding hands, dreaming of the future; it was all so tender and sweet and, of course, naive. Just like the Hollywood movies we would sometimes go to see. In a dark movie theater, watching Fred Astaire twirl Ginger Rogers (in a satin, feathered gown of course!) around the ballroom floor, you could almost forget that anything horrible was happening elsewhere in Europe.

But that life of not knowing is long gone and so are the people I loved back then: my parents, my sisters and brother, so many aunts and uncles and cousins, neighbors and friends.

How did it all race by so fast? This is a question you, too, will ask yourself if you get to live as long as I have.

I am almost 92 years old but I sometimes still feel like the young girl who was in love with the Danube and the dancing lights and moonlit ballrooms on a black-and-white screen.

I don't know why I've outlived everyone (and neither will you, I am sure, if you are so blessed.) Why did I get to live so long when so many others were denied that privilege? That is another 'why' that I cannot answer.

Perhaps it is *Bashert*, I was meant to live this long so that I can now testify for all those I left behind.

This is my story. It all happened more or less the way I am about to tell you, or at least, this is the way I remembered it when I still could.

PREFACE

Putting My Mother's Words
in Context

By David Rich

I was a kid in the early 1960s when my mother first began working on her "remembering" tapes. No more than 11 or 12, but I have memories of hearing her speaking into that little tape recorder my father bought. In the evenings, when we were supposed to be asleep, my mother went up to her bedroom and began speaking into the recorder. Sometimes my brother and I would sneak out of our room and stand by her door, trying to listen to what she was saying. Mostly she was speaking Hungarian or Yiddish, languages my older brother understood better than me. (He was born in Europe, when my parents were still in a displaced persons camp.)

She would speak into the recorder when she was not too tired from her busy days of working in my father's office and taking care of our house. When she was not recording, she spoke very little about her life before coming to America. Sometimes she'd mention her parents or her family in the old country but mostly she'd say that the past was the past and that talking about it was too difficult.

"I am done with remembering," she would say when we were teenagers and wanted to ask her questions. She told us that if we were really interested, there were plenty of history books to read. Perhaps this was in reaction to my father, who talked about his five years in Dachau all the time. He had survived because he was a medical doctor and his services were in desperate demand.

But it was my mother's silence that most intrigued my brother and me.

Like most kids our age, war movies and tales of evil Nazis fascinated us. We spent hours looking at the old issues of *Life* and *Look* magazines that my father kept tied up in string in the garage. We were amazed by those gruesome black-and-white pictures of corpse-like prisoners and piles of glasses and shoes belonging to the dead. Equally repelled and awed, we spent long hours talking about the hideous things we'd do to any Nazi who wandered into our backyard. But, even with the photos in front of us, the images represented abstract stories that happened to other people in other countries. We did not connect with the concept that some of the victims in those awful photos could be long lost relatives or friends of our parents. Growing up in New City, New York in the 1960s, we were among a privileged generation of kids whose greatest concern was getting a Hank Aaron baseball bat or finding someone on the block with a color television.

In the early 1980s, my parents were living in Arizona to be closer to the family and, after my father died, my mother rented a small apartment for herself. She put most of her boxes from the house in New City into a storage facility. About three years ago I got a call from the facility telling me that my mother had not paid the rent on the unit for over a year. The contents were to be auctioned off if I did not cover the expenses and claim the items.

I immediately wrote a check and delivered it myself. I was given the keys to the unit and it was then that I discovered my mother's trunk.

I took the trunk home and a few days later, I came across a red scarf. Unfolding it, I found those yellowing onionskin pages, my mother's "remembering binder." I read that night in a kind of frenzy, racing through the pages, unable to stop reading even long enough to drink some water or use the bathroom.

I tried to talk to my mother about the binder pages but she did not remember having written them. By now, Mom was living in an assisted living facility near my house and, though I visited her almost every day, I could tell that she was slipping away. She was healthy and her body was strong but her mind had begun to wander and her doctors had advised me that she should no longer be living alone.

Knowing that I was slowly losing my mother made finding these pages all the more meaningful to me.

On a personal level, I was amazed that this was actually a story about my own mother and the grandparents I hardly recognized. I felt that it was an important document and it should be published. It reminded me that my mother's story filled a vacuum, as not much has been written about the Jews in Hungary during the war.

I've read many books about the Holocaust. As the child of two survivors, those brutal photographs from *Life* and *Look* magazine continued to haunt me even decades later. Thank God my mother was not sent to those camps. Because of her quick wit and her indomitable spirit, she managed to save herself and many members of her family. Her survival was a small miracle in a vast sea of madness. I want the world to know her story. My brother, Joe, believes Mom's story is universal and can inspire anyone forced to deal with hardship.

The day after I read the binder pages, I hired a typist to put my mother's memories onto a Word file. Then I found a writer to fix the language and edit the story into a more readable style. The chronology of her story was all over the map, and I needed someone to make it more understandable. While that was being done, I did some research of my own about Hungary at the Holocaust museum in Budapest and the Shoah Foundation at the University of California in Los Angeles, California.

My wife, Bey, and I traveled to Budapest and spent a week exploring the places my mother discusses in her book. We even visited the apartment building in Budapest where her family had been living before the war. The people now in that very apartment were kind enough to let us wander around the place. Walking through these rooms gave me the eeriest feeling, as if the ghosts of the past were actually still there to acknowledge my visit.

Though much of the city was destroyed during the war, enough of the buildings and bridges remained to give us a visceral sense of the city during those years from the early 1940s, which is about the time frame of my mother's story. I had wanted Mom to take this trip with us but she did not want to return.

"It was difficult enough to get out, why would I ever want to go back there?" she asked with a shudder.

I reminded her that all that had happened more than sixty-five years ago but could not persuade her to change her mind.

Before I found my mother's binder, I knew very little about the war in Hungary, a country that has long been shrouded in mystery. Finding information about that time and place was not easy, even though many thousands of books have been written about the war, including numerous memoirs of the few fortunate Jews who managed to survive the Nazis.

Though I make no claims at scholarship, in order to put my mother's story into some kind of historical context, I want to share some of the things I learned about Hungary both in my research and during my travels.

Following the end of World War I, Hungary was one of the first countries in Central Europe to actually legislate anti-Semitic laws. The Numerus Clausus law of 1920, for example, limited the number of Jewish students who were allowed to attend university. Many other laws against Jews were imposed and yet, until 1944, Hungary was just about the only country within the German sphere of influence that allowed Jews to live in relative peace and to openly practice their religion. Ironically, Hungary was one of the only places in all of Europe where Jewish refugees from surrounding countries were granted asylum. In short, Hungary was an openly anti-Semitic country that protected its Jewish population and took in Jewish refugees when no other country in Central Europe would.

This paradox actually came about in the autumn of 1938. Jews from all over Europe were being forced from their homes without a place to go. In desperation, a group of 250 displaced Jews rented a rusted freighter and sailed the Danube in search of somewhere to live. No one would accept them until Ferenc Keresztes-Fischer allowed them into Hungary on the condition that they didn't stay too long. In other words: you can come in but please leave as soon as possible.

When Poland collapsed in September of 1939, thousands of Poles swarmed into Hungary. My mother recalls this time and remembers the horrifying choices the Hungarian Jews faced. They tried to hide as many exiles as they could but food was scarce and the task of finding shelter and food for so many was daunting. Then, by the spring of 1940, the Hungarian government began prosecuting anyone harboring a refugee. Many of those found guilty were sent to internment camps.

When Hungary entered the war on June 26, 1941, many more anti-Semitic decrees were issued at the insistence of the Third Reich. A month later, the government evacuated "stateless" Jews from the Polish ghettos. Between 15,000 and 20,000 were marched out of Budapest, shot to death in the countryside and buried in a mass grave. Still, the Kállay government in Hungary continued to reject German demands to deport Hungarian Jews and continued to provide a safe haven for more than 800,000 of them.

Jewish refugees from all over Europe kept coming. In the spring of 1942, 10,000 Slovak Jews crossed the border into Hungary. Though they were allowed entrance, they were not welcomed. There was hardly enough room for the Jews already living in Hungary. By 1944, in one small Budapest ghetto alone, some 60,000 Jews were forced into 4,500 apartments, living 14 people to a room. And those were the lucky ones—for a while at least.

"We were afraid to offer help without extracting retaliation from the government," my mother writes. "We did what we could but it was not enough. It was never enough. Was it from an uncharitable heart or self-preservation? I don't know."

An underground network was established to transport some Jews through Budapest. Courageous Hungarian Jews established lodgings for refugees in cellars, attics, stairways and other crawl spaces around the city. "Sometimes, strange people would be sleeping in our cellar," a friend of my parents, also a survivor, told me once. "We were not allowed to ask about them. After a day or two, they'd be gone and we would never discuss them. Then someone else would arrive. It went on like that for some months."

Most of the refugees could not speak Hungarian and this was their greatest threat in trying to live inconspicuously in a strange foreign country. Those who spoke only Yiddish were obviously more vulnerable and were quickly rounded up by the militia. Those fluent in many languages—my father spoke five or six—were much more likely to survive.

Ironically, until the Hungarian government actually fell to the Nazis, Jews were allowed to attend temple and openly practice their religion. In a library in Budapest, I discovered a letter written in February 1944 by a Polish refugee who was amazed to discover well-dressed Jews praying in a synagogue without any interference from the government, a sight she had not seen for years in her own country. She was also astounded to see that the Hungarian policeman wore white gloves. To her it appeared that the war had not yet come to Hungary.

The situation in Hungary changed drastically a month later when the Germans finally occupied the country on March 19, 1944. After that date, the situation for all Jews in Hungary became ever more dangerous. A wave of arrests and new anti-Semitic directives put the Jewish population on alert. Stateless Jewish refugees living in and around Budapest knew from past experiences what was coming and many of them tried to leave Hungary. Unfortunately, Hungarian Jews still believed they were safe and their government would somehow keep protecting them from the Nazis. Tragically and literally, they were dead wrong. Even though the war was lost for the Third Reich, and they knew it, the Nazis kept murdering as many Jews as possible. In fact, the Nazi killing machine kept working until the very bitter end of the war. In the ten months before the collapse of the Third Reich, the Nazis killed more than 460,000 Jews in Hungary. Those who had stayed were doomed.

I try to imagine my mother's life when she was a young woman in her twenties and the lives of the Jews who never made it out alive but my mind reels into some place of oblivion that I can barely comprehend.

Imagine that one day you are exiled from your home and your family; sent to a foreign country where you don't speak the language, have a place to live, or can get the means to work and eat. Perhaps you scavenge and manage to survive. Sometimes you are provided with food or shelter by another human being. Then, on another random day, you are rounded up into a cattle car and either shot right away or taken to a gas chamber.

Or perhaps you manage to survive by doing things you never thought you could. Would you have the courage to survive? Would you have been able to do what my mother did? Or her sister Heidi?

Was it luck or fate that saved my mother? Or was it, as she thinks, simply *Bashert*?

My Book of
Remembering

CHAPTER ONE

~❦~

M y name is Gizelle Kornfeld Rich and I am forty-four years old. I live in a place called New City, New York, where everything is indeed "new." In Budapest, where I came from, we had trolley cars and museums; we had cafes on every corner where we watched people walking by all day and night and listened to the beautiful gypsy music that was always in the air. Here we live on bare farmland that has been cleared down to the dirt. Even the little trees are new.

We came to America to start over and we are living, literally, on a blank slate.

It is the summer of 1962 and I am talking into this tape machine to tell the story of how I survived the war and how I came to be living this peaceful American life with my husband and two boys. I feel as though I've lived two lifetimes, that I was an entirely different woman before I escaped from Hungary in 1944. I wish I could forget that other life but I won't because it would mean also forgetting the people I left behind. And, anyway, it does not matter what I want to remember and what I want to forget. My head is filled with remembering; with thoughts and little moments in time that won't go away no matter what I want.

My husband, Steven, says that if I write it down, my nightmares will stop. He says I need to remember it all in order to forget. If he is correct, then it will be well worth the effort to put it all down in words.

"Where do I begin?" I asked Steven.

"At the beginning, of course," he replied.

I suppose that means when I was born, in Budapest, in 1918. My father, David Kornfeld, was a Rabbi and my mother, Lina, was the kindest woman who ever lived. In any photograph of my mother, she has goodness on her face.

My sister Rose was the oldest child but because she had some disabilities (in the family we said she was "simple"), I soon assumed the mantle of the eldest and most responsible sibling. After me came my sister Heidi and then Emil, the youngest. We lived in an apartment building on Dohány Street, near the twin-spired synagogue on the Pest side of the city, not far from the banks of the Danube. We were not rich, of course not; we were a religious family and dependent upon contributions from the synagogue and the money my father earned as *Shochet* for the congregation. A *Shochet* is a very important man in the Jewish community, as he supervises the killing of animals to confirm they are prepared in the kosher tradition. Without a *Shochet*, there would be no meat on a Jewish table, which shows just how crucial he is. Until the war came to Hungary, we seemed to have enough money to live happily among our family and friends. In my memories from before the war, it seems like small things made us happy back then; it was not like America, where everyone wants to have more, more, more.

It has been so many years since I last saw my father that

sometimes I can barely remember what he looked like. I have one small passport photograph of him that I managed to carry out of Hungary with me.

My father had a full beard speckled with gray. In my little photo, his dark eyes are filled with sadness and longing. Was he always this sad? It breaks my heart that I can only remember him the way he looks in this picture. I have no memory of him with a smile on his face. I remember that his fingertips were yellow because he smoked so many cigarettes and that sometimes he would pat my knee and sigh deeply as if to tell me that life was sad but we needed to endure.

I do not know what Budapest looks like today; I know I will never see my homeland again. Nor do I want to. But in my memory, it is still the most beautiful city in the world. On every corner you would find ornate buildings and elaborately constructed bridges crossing the Danube that were erected centuries ago; the customs of the past and the traditions of bygone generations are all around the city, not like here in New City, where everything is so clean and spotlessly new that it feels like it was built only yesterday. Americans are not burdened by their past or surrounded by ancient memories or memorials to former glory days; they live for the future and that is why my husband and I wanted to come live here when we left Europe.

I try very hard to remember what was in my head as a young girl but, after all that happened, I can barely recall my life as a child. What was I thinking as the war was raging through Europe? My brain starts spinning in circles when I try to remember those days. I was not political, that I know. I couldn't be. Politics was not considered a proper subject for women, much less for young girls. Even so, I was always interested in history; I was interested in all my classes at school, except mathematics, which I found nearly impossible to comprehend. I loved to read! I went to the library every week to find translations of my favorite authors. I mostly loved the English writers—Jane Austen, Charles Dickens, and the Bronte sisters were among my favorites.

I dreamed of being a teacher and working at a university; perhaps even moving to England to study literature. Of course, in my day and time, these were foolish thoughts for a Jew, especially a Jewish girl.

I did not understand what was really happening in my own country but I wanted to. At the dinner table, I would ask my father his opinion about what was going on in Europe but my mother would shush me or tell me to clear the dirty dishes. In the kitchen, she would scold me for pestering my father with silly questions. "Concentrate on finding yourself a nice young man to marry," she would say. "That's what you should be thinking about."

But thoughts of young men and tea parties seemed so trivial compared to what was happening all around me. I remember the summer evening in 1941 when I first heard about "concentration camps." We had a family friend named Béla Stollár who worked as a newspaper journalist and would often bring us news about the war. I greatly respected Béla; he was a fine writer who wrote about the situation of the Jews when no one else wanted to cover such subjects. Although he was a practicing Catholic, he did not believe in the tenets of the Third Reich. Because he was such a good journalist and he had many Jewish friends, we were always worried for his safety. It was not safe for anyone to be associated with Jews in those days.

But Béla and my father had been close friends for many years; they'd actually known each other for decades, even though Béla was considerably younger than my father. Béla's own father had died a long time ago and I think he came to see my father as a kind of surrogate father figure. My mother adored him and, though she did not trust many Christians, she made an exception for Béla.

That summer evening, Béla told us there were rumors floating throughout the city about atrocities against Jews in the German occupied parts of the Soviet Union. The news had reached Hungary from our soldiers who were returning from the eastern front. My father had heard the horrific stories and did not want Béla to repeat them as Papa thought they were either idle gossip or hysterical fantasies. Papa said no one actually believed the reports. "Isn't that right, Béla?" my father asked, but Béla only shrugged his shoulders and looked away.

At home, it felt as though a cloud of hatred was hovering over the city and signs of anti-Semitism began appearing more frequently around Budapest. Slogans like "Jew Business" were painted on the windows of our shops and yellow Stars of David began showing up on our apartment buildings. Even walking down the street became difficult, as more and more frequently our Christian neighbors openly taunted us. It was terrifying to see the hatred in their faces. Why had they turned on us like this? Only a few years before we had lived together in neighborly peace.

Of all the children in my family, my younger brother, Emil, had the hardest time among the young Aryan bullies. Emil was a slender boy, sensitive, and with an artistic nature. He loved to make model boats and paint watercolors of flowers for my mother. Emil pretended to be brave but I knew he was frightened of the gangs of boys on the street who'd always single him out, calling him "Jew boy" or "animal" and even more despicable names.

I tried to be with Emil whenever I could. I thought I could protect him on the street or least make sure he did not fight back when he was teased. Fighting back was useless against bullies, especially when he was so small and so outnumbered. I would pull Emil aside and tell him to ignore the boys and their terrible slurs. "It is only words, Emil," I would tell him as we hurried down the street. "It doesn't mean anything."

But, of course, it meant a lot. I was lying and Emil knew it.

Once the refugees began pouring into Hungary, it became harder and harder to find food. Money was even more scarce and, though my father tried to help as many displaced Jews as he could, there was barely enough food on the table for the family. I took whatever work I could find to help at home, jobs working in shops when I could or doing needlework for wealthy Christian women. Heidi and I labored in a linen factory whenever they would hire extra help. It was not easy to find employment but I was resourceful and felt an obligation to help out the family as much as possible.

Every day there would be terrifying rumors or reports about what was happening to the Jews in Germany or Poland. The stories defied belief and my parents tried to shield us from the most gruesome. My mother did not want anyone to talk about the war at the dinner table. She thought that if she kept up with the family traditions that had been ingrained in her since she was a young girl, then maybe the world outside our apartment would stay away. If you did not talk about bad things, if you did not acknowledge them, then they did not exist. (Jews, especially Jewish woman, were superstitious like that.)

My mother spent most of her time in the kitchen, cooking from early morning to late at night. The mouthwatering smells of fresh challah baking in the oven or a huge pot of soup simmering on the stove always filled the house. Friends were welcome, even when food was scarce. It seemed as though my mother could always throw another potato into the pot to accommodate all of the congregants in my father's temple whenever they came to call. I do not know how she did it. I also can't imagine how she managed to keep a smile on her face and pretend nothing was wrong through all the worst of those years. I know she felt she needed to be strong for her family; I just do not know how she managed to do it.

Like my mother, I tried very hard to not think about what was happening to Jews across Europe. I suppose now that it was wrong to insulate ourselves from the outside world but I think that was the only way we knew how to survive.

Before I became really conscious of what was happening in the world I know that, like most girls my age, I was vain and thought a lot about inconsequential things like clothes and books and movie magazines. I always had a good figure and I liked to dress well. (I still do!) Though I mostly had to make do with second-hand clothes from my mother and my many cousins, everything I wore was always clean and pressed and, I made sure, fit me well. Being adept with a needle and thread made it possible for me to tailor my clothes perfectly.

Then one afternoon, in a bookstore on Szables street, I met Imre Danko and we began seeing each other quite regularly. Imre was tall and handsome. He had dark black hair which he wore slicked back in a Clark Gable kind of way. He had deep blue eyes and a little cleft on his chin; I thought he looked like Robert Taylor, the American movie star. Imre had big hands with neatly filed and polished fingernails and, like me, he liked to dress well. His suits came from the finest haberdashery in Budapest and he often wore blue shirts and deep blue ties that matched the color of his eyes.

Imre was the son of a wealthy businessman, one of the richest Jewish families in Budapest. His father's family had owned and operated a successful import operation for many generations. This made him all the more attractive to my mother, who hoped Imre and I would marry someday soon. Like Jewish mothers everywhere I suppose, she desperately wanted me to marry well. I suppose I wanted the same thing, though I was not entirely sure whether I mainly thought about marrying Imre just to please my mother. I adored my mother and would do almost anything she asked.

Though Imre would take me to cafes and lovely restaurants and we would have a good time dancing, I found myself a little bored when we were alone together. He liked to talk about himself to the exclusion of almost everything else and I wondered what a life with him would actually be like after a couple of years. But, for a poor girl like me, was this a real reason to stop seeing him? When I tried to explain my feelings to my mother, she would wave her hand and dismiss what I had to say.

"Being bored should only be your worst problem in a marriage," she told me more than once or twice.

And, in truth, I was flattered by Imre's attention. He was handsome enough to attract admiring glances wherever we went and he danced so well that I knew the other girls at the afternoon tea dances were envious of me when we were together. When I went out with Imre, I was glad I could make my mother happy, my father proud and, truthfully, my sisters a little jealous.

So that, I am a little ashamed to admit, was really what was on my mind as the world I knew was about to spin recklessly out of control. I should've been listening to the conversations swirling around me, in my very own house, when friends of my father would take over the dining room table. They'd come to the house at all hours of the day and night. As the home of the Rabbi, the head of a small congregation, our house was always crowded and noisy. People wanted to ask my father's opinion about everything and anything, about politics and personal problems. He was the Rabbi, so his door was always open.

The men would sit in tight circles around the dining room table or in the living room, always speaking in low urgent voices not meant for the ears of women or children. My father would pass around a bottle of strong liquor and smoke clouds from cigarettes would billow up and hang like a gray cloud in the air.

Like my father, most of the men who came to visit had long beards speckled with gray and they all dressed in traditional dark Orthodox clothing. Other than helping my mother serve tea or cakes to the visitors, I paid little attention when the men were in our house, except when Béla Stollár came to call. He often shared Shabbat dinner with the family. My mother thought Béla was far too skinny and was always on a mission to fatten him up.

The whole family adored Béla. My younger sister Heidi had a mad crush on him, though she'd deny it when we teased her. Heidi was a precocious teenager with a wild fantasy life. Though Béla was twice her age, she imagined that one day he would fall madly in love with her and together they'd fly off to live a Bohemian life in some Parisian garret. I can never forget how animated her face would become when Béla came into the house. Even Emil thought Béla was something of a hero, the way he wrote about the Third Reich and criticized the Horthy government. Things like that took great courage in those days.

When Béla joined us for dinner, the usual restrictions about political discussions were not enforced. We all wanted to know what Béla had learned in his travels so it was impossible not to talk politics around him. As a Christian journalist he had access to more information than anyone else we knew.

I think the first time I became actually aware of any immediate and impending danger to me and my family came one night when Béla was having Shabbat dinner at our house. We had not seen him in many weeks, as he'd been traveling for work and had just returned from a conference in Klessheim, a town just outside Salzburg, Austria. The Schloss Klessheim was a regal palace, reportedly very splendid and beautiful, and was often used by the Third Reich for conferences and to host various guests. After we'd had our soup, my mother asked Béla about his impressions of the city.

"I'm afraid that I wasn't able to do much sightseeing, Lina," Béla replied, wiping the corner of his mouth with a napkin. "Covering the conference took up all of my time."

My father nodded his head. "And what came out of the conference?" he wanted to know.

Béla took a deep breath and exhaled slowly. "Most of it was behind closed doors, of course. Unfortunately, I'm not privy to the actual inner workings of the Third Reich," Béla said with a shrug. "However, rumor has it that Hitler is not pleased with Regent Miklós Horthy's refusal to send Jews to work in German factories, so he's sending Adolph Eichmann of the Gestapo to oversee the deportation."

"Deportation?" my father asked in such a barked response that everyone stopped eating and turned to him. It was the first time in my life that I saw actual alarm in my father's face.

Béla nodded gravely as he stared into my father's eyes.

Everyone remained silent at the table as the implication

of Béla 's news sank in. Up until now, Hungarian Jews had been more or less protected by Horthy's government. We knew that Jews from Poland and other countries had been deported from their homes to work in German factories but we thought we'd been spared that fate.

Could Horthy stand up to this Eichmann?

We may not yet of known about Adolph Eichmann but it was clear from the strained silence that both my father and Béla were aware that something major had happened.

We would soon realize—almost immediately in fact—that no one in all of Hungary could stand up to Adolph Eichmann.

Chapter Two

⁓⫯⁓

Our dinner conversation about Eichmann was interrupted by the arrival of Imre, who swept into the dining room with his usual exuberance, kissing my mother loudly on the cheek. She pushed him away with a wave of her hand but it was clear that she was flattered.

"Imre! Welcome," said my father. "Have you met our friend Béla Stollár? Béla, this is Imre Danko, a friend of our Gizi's."

Béla extended his hand and the two men shook.

"He's Gizi's boyfriend!" exclaimed Emil (to my utter horror!) "He's a university student and his parents are rich!"

I am sure my face turned a million shades of red. I slapped Emil on the head while both Béla and Imre shared a laugh at my expense.

"Hush, Emil," my mother said without a trace of real reprimand in her voice, "you're embarrassing your sister."

"Mr. Stollár, it is a pleasure to meet you," said Imre. "I've read your articles and am an admirer of your work."

"And I've heard good things about you, too," Béla said. "Tell me, what do you do, young man?"

"Well, I recently joined my father's business. We are importers," Imre explained, taking a seat at the dinner table and popping a piece of challah in his mouth. "Though we've suffered with all the recent anti-Semitic restrictions, business has recently improved a little."

"I am glad to hear that," Béla replied.

"And where are you taking my daughter this evening?" my father wanted to know.

"There's a band playing at the Centrál Café so I thought we'd do a little dancing," Imre said.

"Ah, a café!" my father exclaimed, as if this was something entirely out of the ordinary. "That's a very good place to pose a certain question to our Gizi!"

Now it was Imre's turn to blush.

I could barely stand it one more minute. "Come on, Imre, let's go," I said, grabbing his arm before he could respond to my father. "It was lovely to see you again Béla. Good night all. I won't be late, mama. Don't wait up." With that, I hurried Imre out of the house and onto the street.

He was quiet as we walked toward the café and I was too mortified at my family's behavior to say anything.

We finally arrived at the café and were seated near the band. We ordered coffee as we watched the band set up their instruments.

"Mr. Stollár seems very nice," Imre said once our coffee had arrived.

"Well, my sisters think the world of him. I do believe Heidi expects him to be her boyfriend one day."

"And you?"

"He's a good friend to my father and he cares about the Jews. I admire the work he is doing on our behalf."

"Do you admire him as much as you admire me?" Imre asked.

I thought this was a strange question and hesitated a moment before answering. "Well, you are two very different people."

The silence between us seemed as heavy as a wool blanket. Imre looked over to the band. "Looks like it will be some time before we can dance," he said, trying to change the subject.

"Please forgive what my father said tonight," I said, by way of an apology. "He didn't mean to put you on the spot. He seemed so anxious tonight. Darling, look, I know that you are making a good living now with your father and I am proud of what you've accomplished. I think your family is, too."

"They all think it's time I settled down and started a family of my own," Imre said, without looking at me.

Now I was the one who looked away. This was not a topic I wanted to discuss. If Imre proposed to me that night, I was not at all certain whether or not I would accept.

Just then the band started playing a soft Gypsy waltz. Imre held out his hand and I stood up. "I suppose that's my cue," he said as we walked onto the dance floor. I think we were both grateful for the distraction from the uncomfortable topic of our conversation.

The next morning, I could hear my sisters talking as I came down the stairs for breakfast.

"Gizi did not get home until really late last night. I wonder if her date went well," Heidi said.

"I know exactly when she got home," my mother replied. "You'd do well to mind your own business and get yourself ready for work."

"But Mama, do you think Imre proposed?" Rose wanted to know.

"Imre will do what Imre wants. Now, both of you, leave Gizi alone and let her live her life."

I had to laugh. "My whole family is conspiring against me!" I exclaimed as I entered the kitchen.

"I can't take the suspense!" Rose cried. "What happened last night?"

"Yes, please tell us! We can't stand it!" Heidi added.

I purposely took my time getting my coffee and sitting down at the table. I took a sip of coffee before I spoke. "It was just a date," I finally said with a shrug.

"Nothing out of the ordinary?" Rose asked. "No ring?"

"No."

"But I thought he was going to propose," Heidi whined.

Just then Emil swept into the room. He ran up to me and pulled me into his arms as if we were at a dance. He waltzed me around the kitchen. "So when will be have the wedding! My beautiful sister will make a lovely bride," he said with a laugh.

"Put me down, you devil!" I squealed.

"Emil, stop that nonsense," my mother said.

Emil stopped dead in his tracks and looked around the kitchen with the most bewildered expression on his face.

"Imre didn't ask her," Rose explained.

Emil grabbed my left hand. "But I thought..."

"I wish Béla would give me a ring," Heidi sighed.

"You silly girl," Rose responded. "I've told you a hundred times that Béla has no interest in little girls!"

"You just want to keep him for yourself," Heidi spat back.

"Girls, stop this nonsense," my mother said, rising from the table and collecting the dishes. "Gizi's day will come and so will yours, I am sure. Now, come on, it's getting late. If you don't leave, you'll all be late. Emil, have you done your homework?"

As we all got ready to leave I gave my mother a kiss. I had some money in the palm of my hand, which I slipped to her so that the others would not see. "For dinner tonight," I whispered. "And tell Papa he still has his little girl."

My mother hated to take money from me so I always tried to hide it from the others in order to save her the embarrassment.

"You shouldn't have to give me your own money," she said in a low whisper, "but thank you my darling girl." She put the money in her pocket and gave me a kiss on my cheek.

With that, my sister Heidi, my brother Emil and I all left the house together, the same way we'd done on hundreds of other days. I thought this was nothing more than a typical morning for us; the usual banter, teasing and joking.

Little did I know that our lives were about the change irrevocably and forever in less than a few hours.

Chapter Three

Emil ran ahead while Heidi and I walked arm in arm, chattering away. I suppose we were talking about Imre, or perhaps Heidi's crush on Béla, but I really can't remember. What I do remember is becoming aware of a military convoy of cars and trucks loaded with Nazi officers and Arrow Cross soldiers. Suddenly, we seemed surrounded by the Hungarian military and German infantry.

The trucks pulled up and stopped on the street as the soldiers jumped out and began erecting barricades, blocking off streets to certain neighborhoods. Other troops had cans of yellow paint and were painting Stars of David on various stores. Soldiers then went into the stores and dragged out the shopkeepers. People were screaming and the panic in the air seemed almost palpable. Heidi and I clung to each other; we were terrified.

One of the shopkeepers, Lazlo the butcher, was thrown out into the street and beaten. Blood began gushing from a head wound. People on the street stood around but none of the pedestrians seemed able to move. Though it was happening right there in front of our eyes, we could not accept the reality of it.

I grabbed Emil and Heidi and pulled them into an alcove. I did not know what was happening but I realized that it was dangerous to be standing on the street without any cover. The soldiers seemed to be randomly targeting people without any kind of warrant or papers.

I held Emil firmly by the shoulders and shook him. He had a glassy look in his eyes and was staring out into space. "Emil!" I screamed to get his attention over the noise of the street, "Run home and tell Papa what is happening!"

Emil looked at me for a second as if he did not understand what I was saying so I shook him again. He seemed mesmerized by the brutality on the street and I did not think he could speak at that moment.

I repeated my instructions for him to run home to Papa. I was terribly afraid that my parents would leave the house and walk out into this mayhem. Emil was small but he was very quick, I was sure he still had time to get past the convoys and into our apartment building, which was now closed off to traffic by a barricade of wooden crates. "Don't think about anything else. Quick! As fast as you can, get home!"

With one last glance at the soldiers and their trucks, Emil nodded at me, turned and ran down the street.

I remember that moment to this very day and I relive it in my nightmares. How I wish Heidi and I had gone with Emil but at the time I thought we might not make it. I don't know if I did the right thing. All I know is that Heidi and I stood there on the street and sealed our fate for better or worse.

Heidi was kind of hiding in the alcove with her mouth half opened. Her eyes were glassy and beads of sweat formed on her forehead. Her hands felt cold and clammy to the touch. I thought she might be in some kind of shock. I stood in front of her as if I could protect her with my body.

The soldiers continued to pull people off the street, pushing them into the trucks. A red-haired woman in her early thirties tried to break free from a soldier who was holding her arm. She was thrown to the ground. The soldier stomped on her outstretched hand, breaking several of her fingers. She screamed in pain.

Though I was horrified at the spectacle taking place in front of me, my only real thought was that I had to get my sister to safety. I was the oldest and many times I'd promised my mother that if anything ever happened to her, I'd look after my brother and sisters. I had to take charge of the situation. Though my hands were trembling, I forced myself to take a deep breath and try to come up with a plan of action.

I realized we had to get off the street. There were soldiers everywhere but I waited until the ones closest to us had turned their backs and were facing the opposite direction. Then I grabbed Heidi's hand and pulled her down an alley to a cross street.

We ran down to Csányi Street but there I saw another truck and more Nazi soldiers pulling Jews from their shops and shoving them into trucks. We turned and ran in the opposite direction, down several more streets towards Karoly Kiraly Square. Over and over, we saw the same scene repeated. It seemed as though the Nazis were everywhere and they were hell bent on rounding up as many Jews as possible.

I did not know it then, of course, but I later discovered that this was the day—March 19, 1944—the Germans officially occupied Hungary.

Heidi and I rounded a corner on Kiraly Street and spotted a squad of troops moving towards us. We turned to run in the other direction and saw the Chain Bridge, so we crossed over to the Buda side of the city. We were out of breath and slowed down a little when we saw another squad approach us. Heidi began to whimper in desperation and I thought we were going to be caught at that moment. We had no place to run. Then, from behind us, we heard a door open and we experienced our first miracle.

I turned and looked into the eyes of a tall, bald man wearing a pharmacist's coat. "In here!" he hissed, pulling us into his pharmacy. "Quickly! Act as if you're buying something. Don't look out the window!"

Heidi and I did exactly what we were told. The pharmacist pretended to arrange some boxes of cotton balls while Heidi and I moved further into the back of the shop. Two employees behind the counter were looking at us as we walked down the aisle. I could almost feel the hatred in their eyes.

We had our heads bent over the stacks of bottles and other goods. The labels were swimming in front of me and I felt very light-headed. I feared for a moment that I might faint on the spot where I stood.

Despite the pharmacist's warning, I could not stop myself from glancing out the window. A soldier was passing by and I caught his eye. I quickly looked away. I picked up a bottle of something and pretended to be examining it. In a mirror at the back of the shop, I could see the reflection of the soldier outside as he gestured to a squad sergeant. Then the two of them were standing together talking in front of the shop.

My heart was pounding so loudly in my chest that I was sure everyone in the pharmacy, and even the soldiers outside, could hear it. I don't think I'd ever been so terrified in my entire life.

In the mirror I watched the two soldiers talk and gesture with their hands. They pointed up and down the street, then turned and walked away.

I thought, at that moment, that my knees would buckle under me but I forced myself to take a deep breath and remain standing on my two feet. I looked over at my sister. Heidi had tears streaming down her face, which she was trying to swipe away with her hands.

The pharmacist walked back over to us, glancing at his two employees who were staring at us and whispering together.

Then he gestured for us to move into a secluded corner of the shop where we could not be seen by his employees.

"Thank you," I said to him.

He waved off my words. "The radio just reported that Hitler ordered these troops into Budapest. Can you believe it? Into Budapest!"

"But why?" Heidi asked.

"They are to assist in moving Jews to work camps," he shook his head. "But don't worry, my dears. They assured us that Christians have nothing to fear."

"But we are not Christian," I said without really thinking.

"You are Jews?" he asked, his eyes growing wide.

I nodded.

The pharmacist tugged on his mustache as he pondered this news. Then he waved a hand towards the street. "Still, I don't like the Nazi party any better than that damn Arrow Cross."

Heidi began to cry again. "I want to go home," she whispered.

The pharmacist held up his hand as if to stop her tears. "I don't think it's safe for either of you to be roaming the streets right now." He glanced over at his employees. "But you're not safe here either. And I can't let you stay during store hours." He leaned over towards us and, in a soft whisper, said, "You never know who is watching these days."

I took Heidi's hand in mine and, for her sake, tried to sound calm and in control, even though I did not feel either emotion. "You've been very kind," I said to the pharmacist who had surely saved our lives that morning. "Thank you for your help. We'll be fine now, I'm sure."

"But how will we get home?" Heidi wanted to know.

I did not know what to tell her. I glanced out the window. The soldiers were gone from this street but where were they now? Would we find them around the next corner?

The pharmacist put his hand on my shoulder and gave me a gentle squeeze. "If you can't make it home, come around the alley in back when it is dark. My employees will be gone by then. There's a small room back there where you can sleep tonight but you must promise to be gone by first light."

I could not believe our good fortune in finding this man. "Are you sure?" I asked, not wanting to put him at risk but hoping we could accept his kind offer. I did not know what we would do otherwise.

"Yes," he said and convinced me he meant it. "It will be all right. Please. You'll just have to find a place to hide until nightfall."

I thanked him again as Heidi and I left the pharmacy. I checked the alley to make sure I knew where to find the entrance to his back room. It was only just after noon and the sun was shining brightly. Looking up at the sky, I was amazed to see that there were fluffy white clouds in a clear blue backdrop and birds were soaring overhead. It was a perfectly normal sky in a perfectly upside down world.

Where could we go for the next six hours?

As I hurried Heidi down the street, keeping an eye out for any soldiers, I knew there was only one place where we would be safe.

Chapter Four

M y one thought—my only thought—at that moment was
that I had to get to Béla Stollár as quickly as possible.
His office was about a fifteen-minute walk from the pharmacy.

Even so, it took us more than an hour to get there as we
avoided all the major cross streets and kept to the back streets,
racing down the alleyways as much as possible. We had to
cross the Chain Bridge to get to Béla so we pulled our hats
down snugly and kept our eyes focused on the ground. Like
children, we pretended that if we didn't look at anyone, then
no one could see us. Still, the farther away we got from the
Jewish neighborhoods, the safer we began to feel.

I held tight to Heidi's hand and murmured words of
encouragement to her as we walked. "Just a few more blocks,"
I would say to her. Or, "Béla's office is only just up this street."
Heidi bit her bottom lip and did whatever I said. It was obvious
that she was terrified but still, she bravely followed my lead.

Béla worked in a huge office building not far from the
Buda Palace on Castle Hill, which was the Hungarian seat of
power. It was quiet on his street and we raced up the stairs

to his office. Inside, the newspaper was buzzing with activity as we walked thorough the glass doors at the entrance. A radio was playing loudly over the din of the typewriters and conversations. The announcer on the broadcast was talking about the "deportation of Jewish citizens." They seemed to be speculating on what Prime Minister Döme Sztójay would say that evening when he addressed Parliament.

I told Heidi to take a seat in the chair by the wall as I walked over to Béla, whose desk was located by the large window at the far end of the room. Béla was on the phone but he looked up just as I approached his desk.

"Gizella?" he asked, looking confused. I had only visited him once before at his office and at that time I was with my father.

"I'm sorry to bother you," I whispered by way of apologizing for the intrusion.

He quickly made his apologies to the person on the other end of the phone and hung up the receiver. "Not at all, please sit," he said, gesturing to a chair in front of his desk. "But why are you here? Don't you know that the militia has restricted the movement of all Jews? It's not safe for you to be out."

"I didn't know," I said, my voice cracking from the strain of the day. "We left the house this morning and there were all these soldiers and they were pulling people out of their shops. They were throwing everyone on trucks and we didn't know where else to go." I could feel the strength start to seep out of me and I could no longer hold back my tears.

Béla reached over and handed me his white handkerchief. "It's all right, Gizi. Everything will be all right. You said 'we'?"

I used his handkerchief to wipe the tears from my eyes. "Yes. Heidi, Emil and myself."

"Where are they now?" he asked, alarmed.

"I sent Emil home to tell Papa what was happening. I don't know if he made it back safely or not. Heidi and I hid out in a pharmacy. I'm worried sick about Emil. Please Béla, you have to find out if Emil made it home or not. I have to know if my family is all right!" I could feel hysteria rising up in my throat and though I so wanted to be calm and strong in front of Béla, my feelings and terror were overwhelming me.

"Wait here," Béla said and stood up, walking towards where I'd left Heidi. He went over to my sister, took her by the hand and walked her back to his desk. He pulled over another chair from a nearby desk, sat her down next to me and picked up his telephone.

Heidi and I held hands while we listened to Béla speak on the phone. I did not know who he called but I heard him mention my father's name and our home address several times. The expression on Béla's face was completely blank. He waited for a few long moments, listening intently to whoever was talking on the other end of the line. I could not figure out what was being said to him. Fear raced through my entire body. Heidi started to quietly cry again. Béla waited a long time without saying anything before he hung up the phone.

"Béla, what?" I asked, crazy with worry. "What happened?"

"That was my friend at the constabulary," Béla explained in a controlled and steady voice. "They've blocked off your street and many others in your neighborhood. Many Jewish families were taken away; they are to be relocated into several 'ghettos' throughout the city. My friend called his contact in the building next to yours and they ran over to check on your family. Your parents are still there and so is Emil. Apparently, everyone is safe and unharmed."

"Thank God," Heidi cried.

I realized that I had been holding my breath and it was a

relief to feel the air in my lungs again. "We have to get back home," I said.

Béla shook his head is disagreement. "No!" he exclaimed, more loudly than he intended I think. His response had alerted a few of the writers sitting behind him and one of them called out, "Hey! Stollár. Keep it down, some of us are working here!"

Béla motioned for us to stand and he led us to a small storage room in the back of the office where we could talk privately. He closed the door and moved closer to Heidi and me. "It's just come over the wire," Béla said, "Eichmann has been personally selected to oversee the organization of the Jews for deportation. Trust me, the Nazis will not stop to rest. They are machines when it comes to the Jews."

"Eichmann?" Heidi asked.

"SS Colonel Adolph Eichmann, Hitler's personal ambassador and not someone any of us want to be in control," Béla said.

I was confused. I didn't know a lot about politics but I thought I understood a few important things. "But Regent Horthy rules Hungary," I protested to Béla.

He shook his head in frustration, which I knew was not directed at me. "Not any more," he told me. "Döme Sztójay is now the Prime Minister by order of the Fuehrer himself."

"By Hitler?" I asked, not really believing that was possible. "Why would the regent allow that to happen?"

Béla began pacing the small space in the storage closet, raking his hands through his hair. "Horthy's hands are tied. Hitler will cede both Transylvania and Southern Slovakia back to the Romanians if he doesn't do exactly what he is told."

This was the most alarming news of the day, even on a day as alarming as this one. Miklós Horthy had protected the Jews in Hungary and stood up to Hitler many times; Döme Sztójay was known to be entirely pro-German. Who would protect us now? "So our entire country is being held hostage? Is that what you're telling me?" I asked, not meaning to direct my frustration and anxiety at Béla. "This means we'll never get home."

"Sztójay as Prime Minister will no doubt enlist Ference Szálasi and his Arrow Cross party to assist Eichmann," Béla added, more to himself than to us. He was thinking quickly, trying to figure out what this news meant to us.

But I could not accept that the world had changed so drastically in such a short period of time. "This is only temporary," I said to Béla, partly because I so wanted to believe it myself. "Horthy has already sent some Jews to work in the German factories, Eichmann may take a few hundred more but surely he'll leave after that." I was desperate for Béla to agree with me.

He didn't. "Don't fool yourself, Gizi," he said, very gently. "My sources tell me Eichmann has been given this mission for one reason and one reason only."

"Which is?" I asked, afraid to hear the answer.

Béla stopped pacing and stood before us. He took a deep breath before answering. "To bring about the final solution to the Jewish problem," he said in a whisper.

Heidi grabbed my hand and held on tight. We had heard this declaration before, "the final solution," but had barely believed that it actually existed. Did the Nazis really think they could rid Europe of all the Jews? Did they really want to kill all of us? My brain was reeling as I tried to comprehend the meaning of Béla 's words.

Heidi had more practical things on her mind. "What about Uncle Stefan?" she asked. "He always said he'd help us move to Switzerland."

Stefan was my father's brother and he lived right outside Fribourg (in central Switzerland) where he'd emigrated as a young man. He had married a Swiss woman and they owned a small dry goods store. Stefan and Isla weren't wealthy but Stefan had written many times suggesting we leave Hungary and come to live with him and his family. In the past few years, his letters had become ever more urgent as news of the war spread across the continent. My father had insisted that Stefan was exaggerating the danger in Central Europe, especially in Hungary, though now it was apparent Stefan had been correct all along.

"Switzerland?" I asked. The country seemed as far away as the moon. "How would we ever get there?"

"Béla will help us," Heidi said. "Won't you?"

"No," I replied, before Béla could respond. "We can't ask you to risk your life for us. Come on, Heidi, we have to go now."

Béla grabbed my arm. "Wait," he said. "Let's think this through. Surely, you're better off getting out of the country but, until then, there may be a way for you to stay here."

"How?" I asked.

"It's dangerous," he warned.

"Béla, please, tell me what you are thinking."

"All right. First, I'll cable your Uncle Stefan as well as Ambassador Lutz. Hopefully, they can start the process of getting passports for your family to emigrate as soon as possible."

"But what will we do in the meantime?" Heidi asked. "How will we live if we can't even get home?"

I told Béla about the pharmacist and his offer to let us stay in his back room for the evening.

"That's good," Béla said slowly. "But it is only a temporary solution and for one night only. Look, I have some friends who are as opposed to this war as I am. I can't tell you anything more about them but they can make you some papers."

"You mean illegal papers," I said, even though I suppose that was obvious enough.

"Yes, they will be false papers but good enough to fool the authorities and allow you to stay in Budapest."

"These papers will allow us to go home to our family?"

"Not exactly. The papers would change your identity. You can't be Jewish anymore and remain safe. You'd have papers that would change you into law-abiding Christians."

Somehow that concept was entirely shocking to me and my first reaction was to protest. "No, Béla. I can't disguise myself as a Christian. I'd be denying everything I am and everything my family stands for. Have you forgotten that my father is a rabbi? What would he think? I am sorry but what you are suggesting is just impossible."

Anger flashed through Béla 's eyes. "Would you rather be dragged to one of Eichmann's ghettos and be deported God knows where?" he asked. "What's more important, your pride or your life?

"Béla's right, Gizi," Heidi said gently as she stroked my shoulder. "What's so terrible about pretending to be Gentiles?"

"You won't be denying your God," Béla added, his voice softening. "Surely your father would want you to do whatever you had to do in order to survive."

How could I explain that the very idea of pretending to be Catholic was like a knife in my heart? I carried my spirituality inside me; my religion guided and protected me. Next to my family, my Jewish heritage was the dearest thing in my life, the one thing that kept me sane in a world gone crazy. And here Béla was suggesting I toss it aside as if it was nothing more than an old dress I no longer wanted to wear. Was it even possible to change the person you are at your very core? Once you gave that up, what was left?

But Béla, and apparently Heidi also, did not see it as a moral dilemma. For them, the issue was decidedly more basic. "Your choice is to live or to die," Béla said with a shrug of his shoulders. "I know it's not fair, it's not right, but it is as simple as that."

Heidi nodded her head in agreement. "We can hide at night and blend in during the day. Look, we can start by changing our hair." Heidi began wrapping her hair in the style of the braided bun that was the way most Christian women in Hungary dressed their hair. "See? We can do it, Gizi. That pharmacist thought we were Gentiles, and we can fool everyone else."

"Is it so easy for you to deny who you are?" I asked Heidi. "Do you find it so simple to deny your God and switch religions as if you were changing your hair style?"

"Yes," Heidi said without any hesitation. "If it means we get to live; then, yes, I will do whatever it takes. And so will you."

Béla placed a warm hand on my cheek. "Gizi, is your pride worth dying for?" he gently asked.

The world was completely upside down at that moment and so was I. I didn't know what to think or what was right any more. A few moments went by before I could respond. "Do you really think we can do it?" I asked. "Can we really pass as Gentiles?"

Béla nodded his head. "I mean no disrespect when I say that neither of you really looks Jewish."

"You mean we don't have hooked noses?" I replied, somewhat more harshly than I intended.

"Well, then, I am thankful for my straight nose and for yours," Heidi said before Béla could answer.

Still I was not yet entirely convinced. "How long will it take to get those papers?"

"A day or two, maybe three," Béla replied.

"All right, then I don't have to decide right at this moment," I said. I would have to think about the situation long and hard and at least buy myself some time to come to a decision. I was not sure I was capable of pretending to be a Gentile, whether or not it was a good plan. "We have a place to stay tonight. We'll think about the rest tomorrow."

"But your clothes," Béla said. "You'll need to buy new ones." Heidi and I were both still wearing the muslin work dresses and blue smocks worn at the linen factory. He took out his wallet and offered us a bunch of bills. I tried to protest but he would not listen. "Just take the money. Buy the clothes. If you can stay away from the Nazis for a few days, I can get you those papers."

He wanted to know the address of the pharmacy where we would be spending the night. He would come by the shop tomorrow morning to tell us what he'd been able to do about the papers and if he could get any more information about our family.

We tried to thank him for all his help but he did not want to hear about our gratitude. He acted as if he wasn't doing anything particularly special or dangerous, for that matter.

At that moment I still thought I had a choice to make. I believed I could delay the decision about pretending to be Gentile for at least a few days. I still had the hope that perhaps it would not be necessary. I did not know that my fate had been more or less sealed the moment I agreed to Béla's plan.

Before we left the storage closet, Béla opened a file cabinet and took out a camera. He said he needed a photo of each of us for the forged papers. Before he took the photo, Heidi and I rearranged our hair into braids, which we then looped around our heads and secured with pins. Béla quickly snapped two photos.

Our transformation into Gentiles had begun.

Chapter Five

We left Béla's office and hurried through the streets to a department store on Rumach Sebestyen Street, on the Pest side of the city. There were fewer Jews in this neighborhood and it felt safer for us. The store we found was crowded with shoppers. Apparently there were a great many people in Budapest who were unconcerned about what was happening to the Jews in the city. Women in the store examined merchandise and tried on shoes as if nothing out of the ordinary had happened that day.

We followed their lead even though shopping seemed ridiculously superfluous and meaningless to me that afternoon. I tried to think of it as a mission or an assignment. I had a costume to purchase for a part I would be performing, not on stage but in real life. Heidi and I tried to be inconspicuous and blend in as much as possible. I suppose we did a good enough job of it because no one paid any particular attention to us.

We sorted through the racks of women's clothing. I found a suit that seemed to be my size and Heidi bought a dark green dress with a dirndl waist that was the style at that time. We paid for our purchases with Béla's money and left the store with our packages.

A few blocks away, we found an alley and ducked in. Hiding behind a crate of boxes, we changed into our new "Christian" clothes and tossed our old work clothes into a garbage bin. Our disguise was complete and as I took a long look at Heidi, I thought it was possible that we could do this. She looked, well, she looked like all the other Christian women on the street that afternoon and I suppose I did, too.

Despite how we looked, we were still two women without a home to return to. By then, the sun was setting over the Danube and the city glowed softly in an amber color. On any other day, I would have stopped to admire the colors of the sun-streaked sky but this was not an ordinary day.

I wanted to run to the safety of the pharmacy, but it seemed more prudent and inconspicuous to walk more leisurely and to keep pace with all the other pedestrians out and about that afternoon.

When we got to the street where the pharmacy was located, we strolled past the shop and, as casually as possible, peeked into the window. There I saw that one of the employees had not left yet. She was putting on her lipstick and looking at herself in the mirror as we passed the shop. We walked down the street and circled back. As we came down the street, I could see the employee leaving the store. She closed the door behind her, turned to wave at the pharmacist inside, then hurried down the street.

The pharmacist appeared in the window of the shop. He flipped the sign on the door to read "closed" and peered out into the street. I stepped from the shadows and into the light of the street lamp so that he could see me more clearly. I nodded my head at him.

He raised his hand to wave me towards the back of the shop.

I grabbed Heidi's hand and we went down the alley to the back door of the pharmacy. The door creaked open and the pharmacist stepped back to let us in. He didn't say anything but gestured for us to enter. He pointed to a stack of blankets in the corner and, with a tip of his hat, he left us alone in his shop. At the time, I did not think about this extraordinary gesture of kindness to two absolute strangers but over the years, I have marveled at our great good fortune in discovering such a good man at such a critical point in our lives.

Moments after the pharmacist left, I turned to Heidi to tell her I had to leave her alone for a little while. I needed to see Imre. Heidi protested but I was insistent. I thought that going to Imre was the best thing for me to do. I was hoping he would help us and we desperately needed his help.

"I want you to stay here," I said to Heidi. "I must go speak with Imre. He lives quite close. If I don't come back, Béla will be here tomorrow."

Heidi wanted to come with me but I did not think that was a good idea. How would we get back into the pharmacy? She tried her best to talk me out of leaving her but I was out of the shop and on my way before she could stop me.

By now, it was dark on the street and I felt a bit more protected. I kept to the side streets and walked close to the buildings so that I was always on the darkest side of the street.

Imre lived in a wealthier part of Buda, on Szabo Istvan Street, a tree-lined block of single-family houses with one apartment building at the end of the street. Imre's house, at number 563, was about halfway between the cross streets. For several minutes, I waited by the apartment building at the end of the block to make sure that no soldiers were around to see me. Then I scooted up to Imre's front door and rang his bell.

Imre opened the brass door and his face registered surprise at the sight of me. He stepped out onto the porch, quickly closed the front door behind him and steered me into the shadows behind the sprawling oak tree in his front yard. "What are you doing here?" he asked in a husky whisper. "The Nazis are still out patrolling the streets. It's so dangerous!"

I was surprised that he had not invited me into his house but I let that pass for the moment, as there were more important things to discuss. "I had to make sure you were safe," I said. I put my arms around him and hugged him to me. I was relieved to see that nothing had happened to him. For a moment, I felt safe in his arms, but only for a moment.

He barely returned the hug. He grabbed both of my shoulders and held me at arms length away from him. "We were hauled out of our store and into the street this morning," he said, shaking me a little bit for emphasis. "They hammered boards over the doors and painted Stars of David on the windows. They told us that all Jewish businesses were closed until further notice. My mother is frantic; the doctor gave her a sedative this morning."

"And your father?"

"He's badly shaken, we all are. Everyone is scared to death. I don't know what we're going to do." He released me and began chewing on a fingernail.

I realized that he had not asked about my family. I had always had my doubts about Imre and I was beginning to understand why. He seemed utterly oblivious to what I was going through and how much I needed his support and help. If I couldn't turn to him, then who could I turn to?

"Heidi and I were caught on the street," I offered without being asked. "We have a place to stay tonight but tomorrow...."

He didn't say anything. He was looking back at his house

as if he was not even listening to me. Perhaps I needed to be more clear about what I needed from him. "Imre, I don't think Heidi and I can make it back to our house. The streets have been barricaded; we have no place to go. I was hoping we might stay here with you."

He looked away from me and shrugged. "What can I do? My family doesn't....."

Just at that moment, the front door to his house jerked open and Imre's mother appeared in the light of the doorway. She was wearing a housecoat and her hair was sticking out in unruly pieces. It looked as if she had just gotten out of bed. She rushed towards us. "What are you doing here?" she spat at me. "Leave my son alone! Go home where you belong! You'll get us all in trouble by standing out here. Leave! Now!"

She grabbed Imre and tried to pull him up the steps to the house.

"But the Nazis have blocked off our street!" I said, trying to make her understand the urgency of our situation. "Please, we need your help."

Imre put his arm around his mother. "I'm sorry," he said to me, regret washing over his face. "My family needs me."

"*They* need you?" I sputtered, completely confused by his reaction. Wasn't this the man who had talked about taking care of me for the rest of my life? What had happened to all those promises he had made?

As I watched in disbelief, Imre led his mother up the steps and guided her towards the front door.

I turned to leave. I suppose in some way, I had always suspected that Imre could not be entirely trusted. If I had really thought he'd be there for me, I would've brought Heidi along. In truth, I was not certain how he would react to my showing up on his doorstep, especially with my sister in tow.

His actions this evening confirmed my worst fears. "I think that we are done," I told him, "so I'll say good-bye to you and your family right now."

I started walking away but Imre left his mother on the stoop and ran to catch me. He turned me around to face him.

From his pocket, he extracted a small jewelry box. He took out a diamond ring which he placed in the palm of my hand and folded my fingers around it. "I'm sorry, Gizi, truly I am. I wanted to give this to you last night. I don't know why I didn't. Now everything is a mess. Anyway, whatever happens, I want you to have it."

I started to protest but he held one hand over my mouth. "No, don't. It's little enough. Take it, please. You may need it."

The ring cut into the skin on my hand and I clutched it even tighter. I nodded. "I have to go," I said, forcing myself not to cry in front of him. "I have my own family to look after."

Now I knew we would never marry, not after tonight. But the ring would prove useful in the near future and I have never regretted accepting it from him.

Chapter Six

Like a rat scurrying through a maze, I made it back to the pharmacy that night using only back alleys. I was so angry with Imre that I almost forgot how dangerous it was to be out in the streets. I knocked lightly on the back door of the pharmacy and Heidi opened it at once. She threw herself in my arms. Apparently, she had been terrified, sitting all alone in the dark of the storeroom.

We wrapped ourselves in the woolen blankets the pharmacist had left for us and huddled together to keep warm. Heidi fell asleep almost instantly but I could not stop my brain from spinning in a million directions. It was almost impossible to believe that just that morning I had eaten breakfast with my family and we had been joking as if nothing bad would ever happen to us. Now, less than 15 hours later, I was shivering on a hard wooden floor, disguised as a Gentile, with a wedding ring in my pocket and the fate of my family completely unknown. My stomach growled with a hunger so fierce it was almost painful. I had not thought about food all day and now

I wished I had eaten more breakfast. At that moment, food seemed like the most unobtainable luxury in Budapest.

I am not sure if I slept five minutes or five hours or not at all. It was surely one of the longest nights of my life. I know that I was awake right before the gray light of dawn seeped through the cracks under the door. I did not know what time it was or what time the pharmacist would return to open his shop but I realized that Heidi and I needed to be ready to move at a moment's notice.

I shook Heidi until she was fully awake and we used the small sink to splash water on our faces. Then we braided each other's hair and dressed in the new clothes that we knew would be considered appropriate for the roles we were about to play. We neatly folded the blankets back into the corner of the room and waited for the pharmacist to arrive.

We heard a knock and I opened the door to the bright sunlight of early morning. To my surprise, it wasn't the pharmacist at all. Instead, Béla Stollár stood in the alley and smiled gently at me.

"Are you two all right?" he asked.

I nodded, surprised at how relieved I felt to see Béla that morning. "It was quiet here last night but the workers will be back soon."

Béla stepped into the small room and looked at Heidi and me with an appraising eye. "Yes, you've done a good job; those clothes and that hair do change you," he said.

"I'm still me on the inside," I insisted, perhaps a bit too forcefully.

But Béla merely smiled at my remark. "So, I sent cables to your uncle and to Ambassador Lutz. They cabled back that they would both do whatever they can."

"Did you get the papers?" Heidi wanted to know.

"I was only able to get temporary movement permits," Béla said, extracting white papers from the inside of his coat. "They are from the Red Cross."

"Then it's settled," Heidi said.

I took the papers from Béla and held them up to the light. Although they seemed genuine enough and certainly looked 'official,' I was no expert in such matters and could not have chosen real papers from forgeries.

"Heidi," said Béla, "you are now EVA VARGA and Gizi, you are MARIA KOVACH. You are both from the village of Csenger, in the northern provinces."

"I like the name Eva," Heidi remarked, adjusting a stray piece of hair at the nape of her neck and patting it into place. She glanced into the mirror. "It suits me. Don't you think, Maria?"

Maria, I thought, I am now to be called *Maria*. I looked at the papers that had christened me with this new name, *Maria Kovach*. I was reminded of an old Hungarian proverb that loosely translates into meaning that you don't become the person you are meant to be until you rename yourself. Would it be possible for me to assume a new name and not become a different person? How much of who I thought myself to be was determined by my name?

In light of everything that had transpired, I didn't think I had a choice any more. I prayed that God would forgive me for what I was being forced to do.

"I am working on getting you more permanent papers with your photos attached," Béla explained. "But that will take some more time."

"But now we can stay in Budapest, near our family, can't we, Béla?" I asked.

"You can stay in the city, yes but as Christians you will not be allowed to enter the Jewish ghetto," he replied.

I fought back my tears. "So be it," said Maria, the person I would now become.

"Thank you, Béla, we are forever indebted to you," my sister said.

Béla wished us Godspeed as we left the pharmacy. He was off to his office and Heidi and I needed to get something to eat and make a plan for the day.

We found an outdoor café not far from the pharmacy and ordered pastries, fruit and coffee, which we devoured in no time, and placed another order for seconds of everything.

We needed to think about work. We had almost no money left and I did not want to have to ask Béla to support us any more than he already had. For the past few months, Heidi and I had been working in a linen factory near the Tattersall racetrack but it was too dangerous to return there. They knew us as Gizi and Heidi, two Jewish workers. We'd have to find work as the Christian women we'd become. And we'd have to find a workplace where no one had ever known our family or us.

Heidi had just ordered a third cup of coffee when I noticed a tall blonde man looking at me from across the street. I recognized him as one of the foremen at the linen factory. I did not like the way he was staring at me. I remembered him as a short-tempered little man who was always screaming at anyone who took more than their allotted five-minute break.

"Stay here, Heidi," I said. "Keep your head down and don't move. I'll be back in a moment."

I got up from the table and hurried down the street, walking away from the factory foreman. I planned to lose him in the crowded street.

But he crossed the street and followed me down the block. "Wait!" he yelled, raising his hand and pointing in my direction. "Aren't you Gizella from the linen factory? I know you! Stop!"

I turned to glance at him. "No, you are mistaken," I said over my shoulder as I continued down the street. "My name is Maria." I could feel a trickle of sweat down my back as walked.

Coming towards us on the other side of the street was a squad of Arrow Cross militia.

"Wait! Wait!" the man from the factory called out to them. "Officers, she's a Jew! Stop her!"

Just at that moment, a double-decker bus pulled up to the curb and I ran for it. I jumped on the bus and ran up to the top deck just as two of the militia jumped onto the first floor of the bus. On top, I raced towards the back of the bus as the militiamen were just starting up the front steps. By the time they reached the top deck, I was hurrying down the back steps. I jumped off the platform and back onto the street. I lowered my head and crouched down to make myself more inconspicuous among the other pedestrians. The bus pulled out into traffic as I escaped into the crowded street.

My heart was pounding in my chest and my throat was painfully dry as I made my way back to the café and my sister. Another miracle had saved me from being captured.

Heidi had seen what happened from her seat at the café and she was positively pale with fright. I told her to quickly pay the check and we hurried away from the café. We had to find a safer part of town.

We spent the long day wandering the streets of Budapest, unable to find a safe haven anywhere. It was twilight as we walked along the Danube, exhausted and weary. We needed to get off the streets; we needed to find a place to sleep that night.

A group of soldiers walked past us on the street. "Move along, ladies," said the sergeant in the group. "This is no place for the likes of you."

We nodded in return.

"We need to get indoors," Heidi whispered as she looked back at the soldiers.

"Just keep walking," I replied, linking my arm in hers as if we were carefree and headed for a tea dance with our sweethearts. "There are some warehouses up ahead. We'll see if we can get into one of them."

We were in a rough neighborhood of factories and storage facilities, near the docks. I could hear the sound of foghorns in the distance. A heavy dense mist had settled over the Danube and the air was chilly. Somehow we had wandered far away from the more populated areas of the city. In any other circumstance, I would never have been so far south of familiar territory but I tried not to think about that and to focus on finding a dry place to rest for the night.

We approached a deserted wooden shack that was attached to one of the brick buildings. Peering through the dirty windows, all I could see was that it was dark inside. When I put my hand on the door, I discovered that it was unlocked and I took this as a fortuitous sign. Heidi pushed on the door and it slowly swung open with a creaking sound. She called out to see if anyone was inside and without any response, she stepped over the threshold and into the shack.

Inside, the storage shack was musty and damp. Only a few dim beams of light came though the dirty windows. In the hazy darkness, we could see that several wooden crates were piled around the walls. As we closed the door behind us, a dog started to bark so I motioned for Heidi to be still while I peeked outside. I could see the shadow of a uniformed night watchman across the street. He carried a torchlight and directed the beam towards us as his dog continued to bark.

The watchman started across the open lot, coming in our direction. The dog, with his big tail wagging expectantly, was trotting ahead of his master.

"Hide behind those crates," I whispered to Heidi as I ducked down next to her in the back of the shack.

We hid ourselves by squatting on the cold, damp dirt floor and curling together against a crate.

We heard the creaking of the hinges as the watchman slowly opened the door to the shack. Moonlight lit him from behind and we could see the shadow of his tall body framed in the doorway. The dog stood next to him sniffing the air. For some reason, neither the man nor the dog entered the shack.

Heidi clutched my arm so hard that I almost cried out. I was certain she would leave a bruise mark on me.

The watchman flashed his torch light in our direction but it was very dark inside the shack and, by some miracle, he did not see us.

"Nothing's there, Wagner," he said. "Come on boy, let's get some dinner."

He stepped back from the doorway and closed the door behind him.

We heard his footsteps retreat into the distance and both my sister and I took a deep breath and sat up.

"That was close," Heidi whispered.

"We have to be as quiet as possible," I whispered back. "Try to find someplace to lay down."

I moved around the crates and, from the left of the shack heard the rustle of some kind of rodent.

"I'll never be able to sleep," Heidi said with a shiver.

At one time in my life, the thought of being anywhere near

or around a mouse or, even worse, a rat, would've terrified me but, in our present circumstances, I hardly gave it a second thought. There were far scarier things I had to deal with just then. It is amazing how a person can adapt to almost anything.

I took off my coat and laid it down near a large wooden crate. "Come here," I said as I sat down, leaning my back against the crate.

Heidi crawled to where I was sitting and sat down next to me. I wrapped my arms around her. "Remember that picnic by the lake last summer?" I said, trying to get her mind off our predicament. "Remember how we laughed when Emil fell into the lake with that huge piece of cake in his hand?"

Heidi pressed herself against me and hugged me tightly. A small sob escaped from her lips. "Do you think Papa will understand what we are doing?" she asked in a weak voice.

I patted her back. "Hush now," I said. "You know Papa would say God has provided us with a way to survive."

"As Gentiles? Do you really believe that, *Maria*?"

I shrugged. "I have to," I admitted. "I have no other choice."

"Maybe God has turned his back on us completely," Heidi said, her voice raw with emotion.

"No, He sees us," I said, certain of that at least. "He is biding his time, like we have to do."

Heidi began to cry and I stroked her hair. I could not stop her tears, I could barely control my own, but I tried to comfort her as well as I could in that dark and damp place. I could not doubt the existence of God, I couldn't; not if I wanted to survive and certainly not if I wanted to maintain my sanity. Most of what I loved had been taken away from me in one short day; I had to cling to something to keep on living.

I told myself I would make it through whatever was coming. I had no choice. At that moment, I accepted my fate. I would be Maria Kovach, I would pretend to be a good Christian woman. I would do whatever it took to survive the war and protect my family.

I prayed that night like I had never prayed before. I asked God to provide for us, to open His heart and show me the way to keep us safe. I might have to be Maria Kovach on the outside but, inside, I would always be Gizi Kornfeld with an unwavering faith in my God and my Jewish heritage.

Heidi's crying finally subsided. I began softly humming one of the nursery songs our mother used to sing for us at night when we were children. Then we sang some popular songs that we had listened to before all of this happened—Heidi had a lovely singing voice. We talked in low voices about what we would do when we got back home. We discussed the food we would cook, the dresses we would sew, the handsome men we would eventually meet, the lavish weddings our parents would make for us, and the adorable children we would someday have. We talked and talked, never above a low whisper, the way women do when they love each other and need to pass the time in a difficult situation.

I knew we'd never be able to sleep that night but, as long as my sister was safe in my arms and we were together, we would make it through the night.

Chapter Seven

⌐⫘⌐

We must have dozed off sometime before dawn. I awoke with deep cramps in my legs. The sun was just beginning to rise and a dim sunbeam streamed through the dirty window. Clouds of dust were illuminated and swirled in the light. The shack and the streets outside were eerily silent.

Heidi was breathing loudly; her head lay in my lap and her left arm was draped across my knees. My back ached from leaning against the wooden crate all night but I was grateful that we'd got through to another day, so I said a quiet prayer before attempting to move my sore limbs.

Heidi began to stir as I tried to ease the stiffness and dampness from my legs. When she opened her eyes, I motioned for her to remain silent. She sat up and I crept over to the window and peered out. The sun was coming up over the building next door and I realized that soon people would be on the streets. It was time for us to make our escape.

Hoping it was safe, I slowly opened the creaking door and we slipped outside without further incident. Hurrying down the street, we brushed the dust from our clothing as we took long deep breaths of the clean morning air. After breathing in the dust and mold of the dank shack, the fresh air was wonderful against my skin and I felt somewhat revived.

We stopped at the first café we found for a quick breakfast of coffee and bread. We had just enough money to purchase another loaf of bread to feed us for the rest of the day. Our plan was to find work that morning. We were out of money and, even more important, desperately needed someplace where we could make ourselves invisible during the day. It felt very dangerous to be out on the street, even with our new identities. I thought about how I was almost captured yesterday and a chill ran down my spine. And walking the streets of Budapest that morning did nothing to allay my fears.

Everywhere we went, on almost every other street corner, we saw Nazi and Arrow Cross soldiers. Squads of them were hard at work moving furniture and other valuables from marked Jewish houses. They loaded up their trucks and carted off people and their belongings. Where were they going? No one seemed to know and I couldn't let myself think about those kinds of questions.

In other places, workmen were erecting massive gates, blocking off entire neighborhoods. Yellow Stars of David were prominently painted on the gates. On the other side of the gates, Jewish men, women and children looked out, bewildered and confused. It was as if they were being herded together like cattle or sheep. I tried to get those images out of my head. I tried very hard not to think about my own family locked behind a gate.

At one point, we found ourselves walking past the Buda Palace on Castle Hill, which was the Hungarian seat of power. Its neo-Gothic facade and sculpted figures of Hungarian princes, kings and historical figures makes it one of the most magnificent buildings in all of Budapest. I'd always felt a sense of pride when I passed this building but today I was alarmed and ashamed. The entire facade was adorned with Nazi flags and that hated swastika, which was the symbol of all that was wrong with the world. The sight made me feel both a surge of white-hot anger and the kind of debilitating fear that left me weak in the knees.

We walked to the Buda side of the city, crossing the Chain Bridge. There were many shops and cafes in the Castle Hill neighborhood so Heidi and I began our search for employment by entering each shop and asking if the proprietors needed any additional help. Over and over we were told that no jobs were available, that there was barely enough business to pay the rent, much less to hire additional help. It was about 2:00 in the afternoon when we entered a rather large bakery and asked if they needed any extra workers. The baker's wife smiled politely at us and shook her head. "I'm sorry, girls. You look like good workers but we have nothing for you today."

I thanked her and Heidi and I turned to leave. Before we could make it to the door, a rather large man wearing a brown suit and carrying a briefcase approached us with a smile on his face. His sharp little teeth were yellowing, probably from the cigarettes he obviously chain-smoked. I had noticed him drinking a cup of coffee and smoking in the rear of the bakery when we entered. He was balding and had such a protruding stomach that his suit jacket was stretched tautly and it looked like one of the buttons might pop at any minute. I had noticed him because overweight people had become something of a rarity in Budapest. Even with the food rationing, apparently some people were still eating quite well.

He stared intently at Heidi as he walked towards us. "Excuse me," he said, removing his fedora as he spoke. "I couldn't help but overhear you asking for a job. Are both of you looking for work?"

"Actually, we are," I said, somewhat hesitatingly. "But we haven't had any luck at all so far."

"Then allow me to introduce myself," he said with a modest bow. "I am Jozsef Fekete, a litigator by trade. My office is just down this street and I stop here for lunch almost every day. This could be your lucky day. I've been thinking about hiring someone. May I ask—what skills do you have and what kind of jobs are you seeking?" He returned the fedora to his head, still staring at my sister.

"Oh, yes, of course," I replied, slightly flustered by the unexpected introduction. "Well, I am Maria Kovach and this is my friend Eva..." Suddenly, I could not remember my sister's new last name. I turned to her and she immediately understood my problem.

"Eva Varga," Heidi quickly said to cover my temporary loss of memory. She extended her hand and Mr. Fekete grabbed it with apparent pleasure.

"Yes, Eva Varga," I said and laughed nervously. "Well, let's see, I can cook very well, do needlework, clean, and do laundry, do almost anything around the house or the garden. Also, I am very good with children."

"And I am very good with numbers," Heidi added, pulling her hand from his grip. "I know how to type and I can take dictation."

Heidi smiled at Jozsef. It was obvious that my sister dazzled him; he had that intense look as if he wanted to grab her right then and there in the bakery. "I recently lost my assistant," Jozsef explained, "so I need to hire someone right away. My wife Janika was helping me with the books and correspondence, but she has not been feeling well the past few weeks so I am without any help at all."

"Then it is fortunate we met," Heidi said. "I am sure we can help you out." She smiled warmly at him. It almost seemed like she was flirting with him.

"Excellent," Jozsef responded. "Eva, you could work with me in the office and Maria, perhaps you could do some housework for my wife. Do you ladies live near here?"

I had to think quickly. I could hardly tell this man that we had slept in an abandoned shack by the riverfront last night. How could I explain that we had no place to stay? Then I remembered what Béla had said about refugees streaming in from the Russian front when our Second Army was massacred in the Don River, just west of Stalingrad. "To be honest with you, sir," I said, "we've only just come to Budapest this morning. We are refugees from the eastern provinces and were forced to leave our homes."

Jozsef raised one eyebrow. "So you need a place to live as well as a job?"

"Yes, well, we…"

He interrupted my response with a quick laugh, as if I'd delivered some delightful news to him. "Our house is only a few blocks away so perhaps you could accompany me home and meet my lovely bride. Everything has to be contingent on her approval, of course. As for your room and board, we have a small room attic that might work as a bedroom," Jozsef offered as he pointed at us. "If you two don't mind sleeping together."

"Not at all," Heidi and I exclaimed in unison.

Jozsef barked another short laugh. "Then come along ladies and let's see if we can't get Janika to approve of our plans." He placed one hand on Heidi's back and gestured down the street with the hand holding his briefcase. Heidi and I snuck a quick glance at each other as we followed his lead.

As we walked along Nagyatadi Street, I could not help but wonder if meeting Jozsef in the bakery was a sign from God that He would provide for us. Was this odd overweight man the answer to my furtive prayers last night?

It only took us a few minutes to walk to Jozsef's multi-story, single-family brick home in one of Budapest's wealthier neighborhoods, on the Buda side of the city. The front steps leading up to the house were swept clean and iron gates encircled the property. The house was painted a caramel color and boasted an elaborately carved archway over the big wooden front door. An antique statue of a saint rested in an alcove halfway up the front of the building. It wasn't actually a palace by any stretch of the imagination but, to Heidi and I at that moment in time, it looked like one.

Jozsef escorted us through the iron gates and up the front steps. He extracted a set of keys from his pocket, which he used to open the front door. We were led into a circular foyer, above our heads hung a crystal chandelier that sparkled in the late afternoon sun. I could only imagine how difficult it would be to dust the enormous fixture, and hoped I would be hired to find out.

"Wait here please," Jozsef said as he tossed his briefcase onto a side table and hurried into the house.

Heidi grabbed my hand and gave it a quick squeeze. The thought that we might have found both employment and accommodation was thrilling.

But after only a few moments, we heard the sounds of arguing coming from the interior of the house and our hopes began to fade. We could not make out exactly what was being said but certainly the sharp tenor of the voices did not bode well for us.

"Maybe this wasn't such a good idea," Heidi whispered in my ear.

"Shush," I said, "I think I hear him coming."

Jozsef came striding into the hallway leading a heavyset woman who wore a dark green housecoat and a great deal of make-up. Unfortunately for her, the dark makeup around her eyes and her brightly rouged cheeks did little to improve her appearance. Her dark blonde hair was tightly braided and wrapped neatly around her head. She had a very large head with a protruding chin and the shadow of mustache on her upper lip. My mother would've said this woman had a "horse-face," a thought that made me smile despite the gravity of our current situation.

Jozsef waved a hand in our direction. "Janika, dear, these are the ladies I was telling you about. This is Maria and Eva. Ladies, this is my dear wife, Janika." Jozsef put his arm around his wife's ample shoulders. "I was just explaining to Janika that you were both in need of jobs and we might possibly work out an arrangement for boarding as well." He rocked back slightly on his heels.

Janika eyed both Heidi and me with a suspicious and coldly calculating stare. She did not seem at all happy to see us in her foyer. "My husband tells me you've both just arrived in Budapest," she said, as if Jozsef had either been lying to her or had simply not gotten the story straight.

She seemed to be the type of woman who needed proof positive of anything anyone said to her, so I extracted our false papers from my pocket. "Yes, ma'am," I said quietly. "We were evacuated when news of the Red Army's advancement reached our tiny village of Csenger near the eastern front. We were told we'd be safer in the city but so far we've been unable to find work or lodging."

I extended my hand with my false papers, as did Heidi. Janika took our papers and walked over to the little lamp on the sideboard to examine them more closely. My heart was pounding in my chest as I could only hope that the papers would pass her inspection. But she hardly looked at them. "Hmmm," she murmured, "did you see any Jews on the road? I'd hate to think our beautiful city was going to be overrun with those peasants."

Heidi shot a quick glance in my direction then looked at Janika. "We were a large group of refugees when we entered Hungary but the Germans stopped us," Heidi said. "The Jews got separated out and marched away. I don't know where they were taken."

Janika nodded her approval at Heidi's news. "Good-bye and good riddance is what I say. I hope they're transported very far away from us!"

Jozsef strode over to his wife and took the papers from her hand. He handed them back to us without looking at them either. "You see, my dear, these ladies are good Christians, just like us!" he said, with enthusiasm. "It would be a sin not to offer them shelter and work during these difficult days."

His gaze lingered on my sister, which Janika noticed. She pursed her lips with a disapproving sniff.

"The Jewish refugees are not unlike us," I said, to divert Janika's attention. "They've also been made homeless by this war."

Janika's eyes opened wide and a spark of interest lit up her face. "Jews!" she exclaimed. "Romanian Jews, Polish Jews, Hungarian Jews, what's the difference you ask? They're responsible for this war, that's the difference. You two are merely trying to get by. It's like our man Szálasi says, 'The return of our aristocracy to power is the only way to bring back national pride.' Once the Jews are gone, we'll have our country back!"

"Janika, please, stop," said Jozsef. "You get too emotional when you start talking politics. It's not good for your health."

"I know very little about politics," I said, "but I agree the Jews have been a problem." In my heart I was ashamed of myself for having made that remark but I knew I needed Janika's approval if we were to be hired. At the moment, my main concern was securing a bed for the night for my sister and myself, even if it meant uttering anti-Semitic garbage.

My remarks seemed to have worked. Janika looked at me as if I were her ally and nodded her head. "I suppose we could convert the attic into a sleeping room without too much trouble. But, of course, we'll have to pay you less to cover the cost of room and board."

"Of course," I murmured.

Jozsef slapped his hands together. "It's settled then!" he exclaimed. "Come inside the house and I'll show Eva the attic. Maria, you take my wife into the parlor and make her a nice cup of tea."

Janika pointed towards the kitchen and I followed her through the house. She showed me where to find the tea and some of the cakes she also wanted, then she retreated into the garden to wait for me to bring her the tea.

My hand was trembling as I lit a match to the cast iron stove. Yes, we had secured a place to stay but at what cost? Had I sold my soul in order to obtain shelter? And would there be a price to pay for my deceit? I would have to wait to see if this new arrangement proved to be a blessing or a curse.

Chapter Eight

Heidi and I settled into our attic room that night with thankful hearts. It had been a long, tense day. My sister had gone with Jozsef to his office, which she said was in total disarray. Apparently, Jozsef's first secretary had maintained an incomprehensible filing system and Janika's work was no better. Eva spent the afternoon sorting through files and organizing invoices. She was exhausted by the time she got back to the house.

My first working day was spent cleaning the kitchen, dusting, changing the bed sheets and cooking dinner. There was one horrifying moment when Janika returned from the butcher with a brown paper package that she tossed on the kitchen table. "That will be dinner for me and Jozsef," she said, rubbing her nose with the back of her hand. "You and Eva can have potatoes and some of those vegetables."

I opened the package to find pork chops and, for an instant, I panicked. Pork is strictly forbidden in a kosher kitchen and I'd never in my life been this close to the meat of a pig. If Janika thought I wanted to share these chops, she was mistaken. I was grateful for a dinner of potatoes and cabbage. I asked forgiveness from my absent father and pretended the pork was chicken when I was cooking. I began to realize that there would be many hidden challenges to masquerading as someone else.

In the attic, Heidi and I slept side by side in a small bed with a lumpy straw mattress. A large wooden crucifix hung over the headboard. The carved Jesus figure had spooky blue eyes that seemed to glow in the dark and iridescent globs of red blood on his body. Heidi wanted to take the cross off the wall but I wouldn't allow it.

The bed was hard and we had only one scratchy blanket but, to us, the tiny, warm attic room was a luxury. After two nights of sleeping on cement or dirt floors in the cold and damp, this musty attic retreat felt like the best hotel on the banks of the Danube. We nestled together in the small bed, our bellies full of potatoes and vegetables and fell asleep almost instantly.

Over the course of the next few days, Janika worked me very hard, but I didn't mind. I was used to hard work and it helped distract me from all my worries and fearful thoughts. There was ironing, sweeping, cooking, cleaning, and dusting to do. If I so much as stood still for a moment, she would assign another task to me. No, the workload was not a problem, but having to spend time with the bitter and angry woman who was my new employer was difficult at best. Janika was one of those sullen, humorless women who only found fault, never pleasure, in her surroundings. She constantly complained about not feeling well, though whatever was wrong with her did not seem to affect her appetite. When she wasn't whining about feeling sick to her stomach, she was ordering me to bring her another pot of tea and more of her favorite biscuits.

One morning, Janika left the house to visit her doctor and

I took the opportunity to call Béla at his office. (I would never use the phone in front of Janika.) It had been days since we'd seen him and I was sure he was worried about us. He answered the phone on the second ring and was clearly happy to hear my voice. I told him where we were staying and how we'd found a safe harbor for the moment.

In addition to telling him about us, I also wanted to know if he'd spoken with my family. He told me he'd gotten word to them that Heidi and I were safe. My parents had been worried sick and Béla assured them that we would be fine. My parents had also agreed to immigrate to Switzerland, if that could be arranged. Meanwhile, Béla was first working on getting them into a safe house in Budapest through the Swiss embassy, which maintained a few buildings for their protected citizens. Béla had even spoken with Ambassador Carl Lutz, who reaffirmed his commitment to helping my family. I breathed a sigh of relief and thanked Béla before hanging up the phone. Without that worry on my mind, I focused on my housework. I wanted to be the best housekeeper in all of Budapest in order to ensure that my job was secure and that Heidi and I could continue hiding with the Feketes.

For a week or so, my sister and I went about our new jobs as best we could. Heidi had reorganized Jozsef's office and was proving to be a good secretary. Joszef seemed pleased with her work and told her so many times a day. Janika did not praise my work but she didn't complain about it either. Mostly she was concerned about herself and her new "condition" as she called it.

After her visit to the doctor, she learned she was pregnant. It was her first child and apparently she had tried to get pregnant for a number of years. For a few days at least, she seemed happier than when we first arrived at the house. The doctor had prescribed some medication for her nausea and she had taken advantage of the news of her condition to spend a lot more time in bed. I was glad because that kept her out of my way and I figured she'd need even more help as her pregnancy progressed. She was definitely not one of those women who soldier through their nine months without complaint.

One morning I was working on replacing a set of buttons on one of Janika's blouses when the doorbell rang. I put the blouse on the kitchen table and went into the front hall.

Opening the heavy door, I was delighted to see Béla standing on the stoop. Other than Heidi, I had not seen a familiar, friendly face in a long time.

"Béla!" I exclaimed with a laugh. "How wonderful to see you!"

I stepped outside and we hugged each other.

"Can you come to the park with me?" he asked.

"I don't know, let me check with Mrs. Fekete."

Janika had come out of her bedroom at the sound of the doorbell. She stood in the foyer in a lacy bathrobe. She held a pair of knitting needles in her hand and a small ball of wool. "Who's at the door, Maria?" she wanted to know.

"It's a friend of mine," I said. "Would you mind if I took an hour to go for a walk with him?"

Janika frowned. "A friend?" she asked, as if she could not imagine I had a friend in the world. She stepped into the foyer and came to the front door to see for herself.

I realized she would not let me leave without meeting Béla so I signaled for him to come into the house and I introduced him to my employer.

"It's a pleasure to meet you Mrs. Fekete," Béla said and beamed a charming smile at her.

Janika blushed with delight. "The pleasure is all mine!" she exclaimed. "Béla Stollár indeed. I've read your stories in the papers. You are a wonderful writer and my father has often mentioned you and your work."

"Your father?" Béla asked politely.

"Why yes. You must know him, Gustav Rigo?"

Béla raised one eyebrow in surprise. "Rigo? The senior counsel for the Arrow Cross? Yes, he's quite well known to me."

Janika missed the sarcasm in Béla's voice. She seemed pleased at the recognition. "He is quite influential, as you know," she bragged. "But how did you meet Maria? She's only been in Budapest a few weeks and she hardly ever leaves the house."

I grabbed Béla's hand and started towards the front door. "We met outside church on Sunday," I lied. It seemed as though lying was becoming more and more natural and spontaneous for me. I grabbed my coat from the hall closet. "We won't be gone long, Mrs. Fekete."

Before Janika could stop us, we were out the door and down the front steps. "It was nice meeting you, Mr. Stollár," Janika called out as we made our way to Béla's car. "I'll be sure to tell my father you stopped by."

Béla waved to Janika before he got into the car and we pulled away from the curb.

We drove to Varosmajor Park, which displayed the most beautiful ancient elm trees and brightly colored flowerbeds in all of Budapest. I had always loved this park. Originally planted in the late 18th century, the park featured more then three thousand species of plants and trees and was a wonderland for anyone interested in gardening. In this calm and tranquil setting, I could almost forget what was happening in the real world.

The leaves from the giant trees rustled gently in the wind as Béla and I got out of the car. A group of young mothers with children in carriages sat on cement benches. The older children played together and the sounds of their laughter pealed across the park. In the middle of the park was a small pond where my brother, Emil, used to sail his handmade boats. The sight of the pretty park would've have been a joy if not for the Arrow Cross militia who were on patrol and marched around the perimeter.

I took Béla's arm as we entered the park. I was anxious to learn if Béla had any news about my family. "Have you heard anything from my...."

"Shush," he said softly, gesturing with his chin towards a pair of soldiers about to pass us.

I lowered my head as they walked past us and a shudder, like a cold draft, ran up my spine. "They are everywhere now," I whispered, diverting my eyes when they turned to look at me.

Béla nodded. He did not speak again until the soldiers were too far away to hear what he had to say. "Your uncle cabled to say Ambassador Lutz managed to move your family into one of the safe houses that the Swiss are operating here. They are living about two miles from your old apartment building."

I jumped at the good news. The Swiss government had declared certain areas of Budapest as nationally designated territories and, although the people living there were still technically in a Jewish ghetto, they were protected from harm by the foreign government and could not be deported to a German labor camp. "Oh Béla, that is the best news I've heard in ages," I exclaimed, squeezing his arm. Relief flooded over me and I finally felt secure—at least for the moment.

"Your uncle and the ambassador are still working to get

them immigration passports but for now at least, they are all safe." Béla patted my hand and smiled warmly.

Safe! I had never understood the glorious meaning of that word until very recently. Other than leaving Hungary all together, this was the next best possible thing for my parents and siblings. "I can't thank you enough, Béla. Now I have only Heidi to worry about."

"And yourself of course," he added. With a quick glance around the park, he reached into his coat pocket and drew out an envelope, which he slipped into the pocket of my coat. "These may help, they're your new identity papers, complete with photos. Keep them with you all the time."

There were too many soldiers in the park at that moment for me to dare look at the papers but just knowing they were in my pocket made me feel more secure. I began to think that we—my family and I—might be able to survive the insanity of this war. If we did, we'd owe it all to Béla.

"You've done so much for us, Béla, I don't know how to thank you."

Béla waved a hand as if to dismiss my words but he did not stop me when I stepped into his arms and hugged him to me. We remained standing there together for a long moment before he moved me away from him and held me at arm's length. "Mrs. Fekete will have it pegged right if anyone reports back to her that we were seen embracing in the street," he said with a smile.

I didn't care. At that moment, I began to understand how terrified I'd been for the past few weeks.

Béla tucked my hand around his arm as we continued walking back towards his car. He started laughing and I stopped to look up at him. "What?" I asked, smiling at the funny look in his eyes.

He shrugged. "Oh, Gizi," he said, suppressing his laughter. "Of all the people you could've met in Budapest, you wind up working for the Janika Fekete! Only you!" He shook his head. "It was a big risk to have taken up with the daughter of the Arrow Cross counsel," he added as if this was news to me. "Do you ever not do things the hard way?"

Tears came to my eyes. I knew he was joking but nothing seemed funny to me at the moment. I felt overwhelmed with emotion and could not control myself. I dabbed at my eyes with my fingertips. "I didn't know who she was when we first moved in. I've had to play along for weeks. All this pretending is so hard. I've had to cook pork and agree with their anti-Semitic remarks." I shuddered at the enormity of my personal betrayal. "I feel as though I'll never be Gizella again," I said in a low whisper.

"Oh, come on now, I was only teasing. You are doing marvelously well and so what if you had to cook pork!" Béla wrapped his hand around mine and gently squeezed it. "No matter what you have to do or how you have to act, you'll always be Gizi to me," he said.

I gazed into his kind brown eyes and felt a little surge of hope. I wiped my eyes with the back of my hand and tried to smile.

"That's more like it!" he said, patting my cheek. "Anyway, what's done is done and, for now at least, you are safe so I am grateful for that. Let the daughter of the senior counsel for the Arrow Cross feed you for awhile." He took a deep breath and slowly expelled the air from his lungs. His face suddenly went quite serious and his eyes clouded over. "I'm afraid that things are only going to get more volatile for the Jews in Hungary. Eichmann addressed Parliament yesterday and announced he was determined to deny Jews in the provinces their rights as Hungarian citizens. He wants to clean out the entire area. He won't allow anyone to protect them. And despite protests from anyone in Parliament, including our Prime Minister, he remains determined to deport not only the refugees but our Jewish citizens as well. If he has his way, no Jew in the provinces will be safe. Soon the only Jews in Hungary will be those living in the city."

By then we'd reached the car, climbed in and were sitting side by side. My fleeting sense of security had vanished. I believed every word Béla said. As a correspondent, he was privy to Parliamentary meetings that were closed to most outsiders, so he knew things no one else could. He had a grim look on his face as he started the car.

"Then we have no choice," I said as I put my hand in my pocket and wrapped my fingers around my precious new identity papers.

Chapter Nine

I try very hard to actually remember the time I spent in the Fekete house but mostly the days blur together in a succession of household chores and tense moments. Those first few weeks took a great deal of adjustment and it felt as though my brain slipped into some kind of fugue state. I was aware of what was going on around me, of course, but somehow I kept my mind detached from my emotions, which is the only way I know to describe those first few weeks.

During the day I kept my head down, avoided eye contact as much as possible and did exactly what Mrs. Fekete asked. I kept any conversation with her to an absolute minimum, always fearful that some remark would slip from my mouth and give me away. I had to monitor every word I spoke and constantly remind myself to never slip into Hebrew or Yiddish, the two familiar languages we spoke at home when I was growing up. Fortunately, my father had been very strict with all his children and we were schooled at a very early age in proper Hungarian dialect.

Perhaps I am overstating the case because it was not like

Janika ever wanted to actually *have* a conversation with me. No, she just wanted me to listen to her. To Janika I was no more than a servant and a country peasant, not worthy of her attention. She called me clumsy and ignorant and "no better than those filthy Jewish peasants" so many times that I no longer heard her. I soon realized that the best way for me to survive was to block out her words and just focus on whatever task she had requested.

Janika was a lonely woman; anyone could see that. She and Jozsef barely spoke when he was in the house. Jozsef would lock himself in his study after dinner and Janika would retreat to the parlor with some needlework or a magazine. She smoked one cigarette after another and often sipped several glasses of sherry before going to bed. A few times a week she'd fall asleep on the settee in the parlor. Once, around midnight, I gently nudged her shoulder to wake her up and tell her it was time for bed but she gave me such a scolding—insisting that she wasn't asleep but just resting her eyes—that I never again attempted to wake her. After that, I said nothing when I found her asleep on the parlor couch in the morning.

She had a few female friends her age. Perhaps because I was instructed over and over by Janika to always address the ladies by their married names, I can still remember them—Mrs. Emil Gál, Mrs. Ferenc Perepatits, Mrs. Laslo Bajsy, Mrs. Pál Nagy. They were all heavily perfumed young mothers married to men who held important positions in the government or the military. The ladies, dressed in feathered hats and wearing snug-fitting tailored suits or colorful spring dresses, would come to the house once or twice a week to play cards or sip tea and sherry and laugh about the latest gossip. They talked about Janika's pregnancy and their children, as mothers everywhere are wont to do. The odd thing was that the war—swirling right outside the front door—didn't seem to have much effect on these ladies; they talked about shopping and new shoes as if nothing else was happening in the world. Once or twice, I heard someone mention Adolph Eichmann and the fine job he was doing by rounding up and deporting the Jews. They all seemed convinced that once the Jews were banished from Hungary, the country would return to the way it was for their parents, when the aristocracy had free rein to do whatever pleased them. From my perspective, it was all sheer madness; these women were reveling in the torture and pain of others as they clutched onto the past and a fantasy vision of their world that had absolutely no foundation in reality. How could they not realize that the world had shifted on its axis and that nothing would ever be the same again?

One day Mrs. Perepatits gave Janika a baby present. Janika was about four months pregnant at the time, just barely showing, but her mood had greatly improved once she got through her first trimester. She opened the gift box and laughed with joy when she held up the gift to show it to me. It was a little rattle decorated with a red and black swastika. "Oh, Maria, just look at what my firstborn will use to play!" she said to me, shaking the rattle merrily in my direction.

I was pouring coffee for one of the ladies and forced myself to hide my true feelings about the despicable Nazi plaything. Janika stared intently at me, expecting some sort of reply so I had to think quickly. "Oh my, how very unique," I offered, saying the only neutral thing that came to mind.

Mrs. Perepatits laughed. "Unique?" she exclaimed. "It's absolutely adorable. The perfect gift for the future heir to the Rigo line." She held up her crystal glass of sherry to toast the future child.

Janika wagged a finger at her friend and placed the rattle

back in its box. "Now Lenora, don't be so hard on Maria. She doesn't have the same taste as we do. She was raised in the provinces. But she's with us in her beliefs, and that is all that matters. Isn't that so, Maria?"

"Yes, ma'am, of course," I replied, turned on my heel and walked towards the kitchen as quickly as possible.

The only time Janika seemed interested in actually talking to me was when she had nothing more interesting to do than sit sipping sweet iced tea or eating chocolates while I worked at some household task. My duties also included taking care of the garden and now that the days were growing warmer, Janika liked to occupy a wrought iron lounge chair on the patio while I tended to the vegetables and flowers. I would have enjoyed the work allot more if I was alone.

When Janika wasn't talking about her plans for her baby, she talked politics and complained about the 'Jewish situation.' Her opinions were impossibly difficult for me to hear so I tried not to listen to what she was saying but I could not block out her words entirely. One morning I was weeding the herb garden when she came out and sat down on her favorite chair. She took a cigarette from the pack in her pocket and lit it with a sterling silver lighter. She filled her lungs with smoke and exhaled slowly. "I just got off the phone with my father and he said that the provinces are free of nearly all Jews," she informed me with a smile of satisfaction on her face. "Once they are done there, they can start working on cleaning out Budapest."

"I find it impossible to believe the Jews were such a big problem that women and children had to be deported," I replied before I could stop myself. I should've known by then that such a remark would only inspire another diatribe from my employer.

Janika straightened her skirt and waved her cigarette in my direction. "Well, someone with your lack of education wouldn't understand," she sighed. "You see, you ignorant girl, the Jews are not just a problem, they are THE problem," she said with emphasis. "They are the reason why King Kaolu was deposed when the Red Army took over."

"But that was decades ago," I protested. "And the women and children have nothing to do with politics."

"The Jews control everything!" Janika angrily replied. "They run all of the banks. They're everywhere: lawyers, doctors, engineers! They control the newspapers. You can hardly spit without hitting a Jew," she huffed, her cheeks glowing with indignation. "Some of us actually remember the glory of Hungary before it was invaded by foreigners and peasants. I know you don't understand, Maria, being a commoner yourself, but trust me when I say that the nobility of this country will never forget or forgive what the Jews did to us."

I turned my face to the dirt and savagely ripped weeds from the earth. As always in these situations, my anger was only mitigated by fear and frustration. I wanted to stand up to Janika and tell her what I really thought of her opinions but I knew I was in no position to argue politics or anything else for that matter. In the back of my mind was always the same question: What would happen to Heidi and me if Janika or Jozsef ever discovered we were Jews? I was both terrified of them and very confused by a God who would put us in such a dangerous and untenable position. Where was that merciful God that my father held so dear? Why had He abandoned us?

I felt the heat rise from my chest to my forehead and knew my face was beet red so I kept my head down and took long, deep breaths. Finally, Janika got bored staring at the back of my neck and returned to the house. As her footsteps retreated on the paving stones, I could hear the distant sound of sirens, the barking of dogs and the screams of men and women being taken from their homes by the militia. That sound was becoming more and more familiar but today it was seemed even louder, closer and more disturbing than usual.

A few moments later, Janika called from deep inside the house. "Oh Maria, come look! It's a parade! Right in front of the house."

I slapped my hands together to remove the dirt and wiped the sweat from my forehead as I made my way through the house. Janika was standing on the front stoop, waving and cheering a contingent of Arrow Cross militia. The soldiers were marching Jewish families down the street. The people carried suitcases and wore heavy coats, even though the weather was quite mild. I could see that many of them were wearing several layers of clothes.

Horse-drawn wagons filled with furniture and trunks clattered alongside the soldiers. Several of the squad leaders approached the Jewish men and women and demanded they remove their jewelry and watches, even wedding rings.

Janika ran into the house to grab her Arrow Cross party flag, which she gaily waved at the so-called "parade" passing by.

"Oh, look, Maria," she excitedly exclaimed. "They've come for those hateful neighbors."

At the house across the street, three SS troopers dragged a young woman out into the gutter. The woman had long red hair and was wearing a white apron. She held a screaming baby in one arm and was holding the hand of a toddler. Her face was a mask of terror.

"It's about time," Janika muttered under her breath.

"Did you have something to do with that?" I asked, frozen on the spot.

"Well, I can't take all the credit. I only *suggested* my suspicions to my father," she admitted with a smile.

The Nazi shoved the young mother and her children onto the truck. The baby fell out of its' mother's arms and onto the street. One of the soldiers grabbed the baby and flung it back into the truck as if it were a sack of potatoes.

My stomach lurched and I had the thought that I should strangle Janika right there on the front stoop. "Why would you do such a thing?" I asked when the breath returned to my body.

"Oh for heaven's sake, Maria, I had no choice," Janika insisted. "It was my duty as a concerned citizen of Hungary."

"They weren't hurting anyone, Mrs. Fekete. They were just trying to live their lives. They are only babies."

She nodded. "Yes, Maria, of course but, you know, from small Jews come big Jews." She shrugged, raised her little flag and turned her attention back to the street.

I could not bear to stand next to her anymore and retreated into the shadows of the hallway. I quickly swiped at the tears flowing down my cheeks and held my hand over my mouth. I bit down on my fingers to prevent myself from screaming out loud.

Standing there in that hallway, I made a promise to myself. I swore to my God that one day, if I survived, I would tell the truth of what I had seen.

Other than those particularly disturbing incidents, most of the time I was strong enough to keep my anxieties at bay, but I would be brought up short at the oddest moments. A memory of my family—a vacation we took in the Alps one year, dancing to gypsy music with Imre, my brother, Emil, sailing his boat in the pond at Varosmajor Park, my father breaking apart a warm challah at Shabbat dinner—a vision would jump into my brain and, for a moment, I became conscious of all that I had lost so quickly and so senselessly. I knew I was one of the fortunate ones; I was relatively safe, as was my family—or so I thought at the time. I had a job, a clean and warm place to live and food to eat. I could watch over and protect my sister. I knew that others were suffering much more than me but, at the same time, I felt guilty for not feeling more blessed and fortunate.

Sometimes I honestly thought that living this deceit was killing me slowly, day by day and hour by hour. Half the time I wanted to start screaming but I knew that once I started, I'd never stop. I began to doubt that Gizella, my true self, had ever existed. It was as if my soul had detached itself from my body and only a shell remained to wash dishes, do the laundry, scrub the floors and agree with Janika Fekete's hateful political agenda. Would I ever again feel like myself? Would I ever again feel a connection to God?

I understood that those questions were a luxury during a time when surviving from one day to the next was the only mandate. While being around Janika was disturbing on many emotional levels, I knew I was safer inside her house than when I was out in the street where I always felt totally exposed and vulnerable. The government had recently circulated a new set of rules specifying that Jews were not allowed to be out doors between 6 P.M. and 8 A.M.; they were forbidden to travel outside the city by rail; all houses of worship were closed; attendance at clubs or social gatherings was prohibited; listening to the radio was even forbidden; and all windows had to be blacked out and kept closed.

Because of these decrees, I was in constant fear of being recognized or stopped by the militia. I did not know if my forged papers would hold up to a close inspection. I tried hard to stay away from my old neighborhood and the streets where I believed my family had been relocated by the Swiss embassy. But in spite of my fears and better judgment, whenever I could get away from the Fekete house, I found myself walking near those forbidden places.

Once, from the behind the gates at Magdolna Street, I recognized Mrs. Leventhal, a neighbor who lived on the third floor of our old apartment building, but I pretended not to notice her. She and many, many others were on one side of a wooden fence and I was on the other.

Arms reached through the cracks in the fence and the distraught people begged for a crust of bread. I was usually carrying groceries when I was out, but Janika kept an eagle eye on every cent I spent and every item I brought home so I could not spare even one item from my bags. I kept my head down and walked pass the gates as quickly as possible. When I thought about my parents or my sister Rose, perhaps begging for food on their street, I'd get so dizzy that I could barely see the sidewalk in front of me.

Heidi was even more exposed to the streets than I was, as she had to walk to Jozsef's office. I constantly worried about her safety during that fifteen minute walk she took every morning and evening. We decided she'd be much safer if she left the house as early as possible in order to avoid running into someone who knew us from our previous lives. Telling Jozsef that she wanted to get an early start on the workload, she left the house the moment the clock struck 8:00 AM. By now, he trusted her with keys to the office. At night, she would stay until it was just getting dark, and then race home. The militia had become very strict about the curfew and being outside during those hours only invited trouble and the possibility of getting stopped and questioned.

Meanwhile, Jozsef assumed a kind of avuncular role around Heidi. He often complimented her efficiency and secretarial skills. At the dinner table, he'd tell Janika that my sister was "a hundred times better at typing and accounting" than his previous secretary. Once he said, "Janika, our little Eva is just a joy to have around the office!" However, since this information was not well received by his suspicious and often jealous wife, Jozsef soon learned it was best not to mention my sister's name in her presence.

When Janika was not around, Jozsef was full of compliments about whatever Heidi was wearing or how she'd fixed her hair. Heidi shrugged off the compliments but I was afraid for her. It was clear that Jozsef was infatuated with my sister. When she'd walk past him in the kitchen or hallway, he had a way of leering at her that I found very disturbing. I worried that before long he'd demand more from her than an inappropriate remark about her body. I thought it was only a matter of time before this infatuation meant more trouble for us.

After dinner one night, when Janika had not been feeling well and stayed in her bed, eating dinner off a tray, Jozsef came into the kitchen after he was finished eating. This was odd enough but then things got even stranger. He walked over to Heidi and held out a little box carved from some exotic wood. It was wrapped in a ribbon and he stood holding it in front of himself like a schoolboy standing in front of his teacher.

"This is for you, Eva," he said, rather shyly, and cleared his throat. He sounded almost nervous.

My sister took the little box and removed the ribbon. When she lifted the lid, gypsy music started to play.

The sounds of that music was familiar to my ears and reminded me of the lyrical sounds that were so much a part of everything I loved about my country, my heritage and my youth. But the source of the music was more than a little disturbing.

A gift? Jozsef was giving my sister a gift? In any other context, this scene would play out like he was courting her, an idea that was simply absurd given our circumstances.

I turned away from looking at the two of them, afraid that my face would register my confusion and fear.

"You once told me that you loved gypsy music," I heard Jozsef tell Heidi as I pretended to be washing the dishes at the kitchen sink. "I saw this little box in a store window and could not resist getting it for you. But, please, my dear child, don't tell Janika it was a gift from me!"

Then he turned and left the kitchen.

Upstairs in our attic room, Heidi showed me the box. "Isn't it pretty?" she asked, opening the lid and humming with the music.

"Oh Eva," I said (we'd agreed to call each other by our false names, even in private.) "You should not have accepted that gift from him."

"He insisted," my sister replied with a shrug of her slim shoulders. "Besides, what harm could come from taking it? It's been a long time since I had anything pretty to look at."

I held my tongue and didn't say anything. My sister was younger than I and I don't think she truly grasped the gravity of our situation. Sometimes I thought our pretense was like a game for her. She once told me she felt like we were playing our roles on stage and one day the show would close and we'd be back to our real lives. I tried to explain to her that this house was no stage; it was all much too real.

Conversely, though, I could not bear to be constantly nagging her about being more careful. She only wanted the things that all young girls want from life—to find a handsome husband, wear pretty dresses, listen to beautiful music and go out dancing. She wanted a life like those she had seen in the movie theater and read about in books before the war started. She could not understand that those romantic stories she liked to read and to see on the screen were not possible for her, not now at least.

Looking back, I can see now that I should have been stricter with Heidi. I should never have allowed things to get so out of control. But could I really have prevented her from falling in love?

His name was Andras Kalman. He was a young Jewish man who operated a vegetable stand near Jozsef's office. Heidi told me about him one night when she waltzed into our room completely flustered yet smiling and excited. She was even humming a song. At first, I was glad to see her so happy. I asked her the reason for her cheerful mood and she was delighted to tell me all about Andras. Apparently, for several days she'd noticed this good looking young man selling vegetables in the street and, that day when she was running an errand for Jozsef, she had boldly walked over to his stand to admire the first tomatoes of the season.

After introducing himself, Andras offered a tomato to my sister and when he handed it to her, their fingers touched.

Andras blushed profusely and started to stutter.

"Something happened between us," Heidi said. "It was like some kind of electricity. I felt it and he did too!"

That is when Heidi noticed the yellow badge shaped like a Star of David on his arm. He explained that all the Jews in Budapest were now required to wear a badge at all times so that the Nazis could keep better track of the Jewish population.

"You must remove it," Heidi told him.

Andras asked if Heidi was embarrassed to be seen with a Jew but she told him that, no, she was only worried for his safety.

"That made him very happy," Heidi said, "because he realized I had feelings for him. He confessed that he had the same feelings for me. He noticed me the same way I had noticed him every day. Oh, my darling sister, I think I am in love. And you should see how handsome he is. He has wonderful smoky green eyes and long dark lashes. One of his eyes is slightly darker than the other. I know he is only a vegetable peddler but I am hoping that Papa and Mama will see that he is a good man, an honest man and a religious Jew, even if he doesn't have so much money. He is so tall and handsome and when he kissed me I felt as though my heart would leap out of my chest!"

"You kissed him?" I asked, incredulous. "On the street?"

"Yes, it was so romantic. I felt like the whole world just stopped for a moment. He held me in his arms as if I was his long lost love; as if no one else existed in the world. And he is a divine kisser," Heidi sighed like the young girl she was. "I wanted to tell him that I was Jewish, too, but then I thought of you and realized that you'd be furious with me."

"You're right about that. Did anyone see you?" I asked, almost afraid of her answer.

My sister lowered her head and looked away from me. "Yes," she said so softly that I could barely hear her. She bit her lower lip. "Jozsef was looking out of the office window just at that moment and saw us. He opened the window and yelled at me to get back to work at once. So I hurried away from Andras and went back into the office. Jozsef was very angry. He grabbed my arm and twisted it till it really hurt. He told me not to associate with those kinds of people. Of course he called Andras filthy names and told me I'd be in trouble if I ever looked at him again."

My mouth went complete dry. "What did you tell Jozsef?" I asked.

Heidi shrugged her shoulders but she could not seem to look me in the face. She stood up and glanced herself in the small mirror over the bureau. "I'm not completely stupid, you know," she said as she picked up a hairbrush began to brush her hair. "I told him I'd do exactly as he said."

"And will you?"

Heidi looked into the mirror and met my eyes in the reflection there. She shrugged and grinned sheepishly. Then she tossed her hairbrush on the bureau and turned away from me. She left our little attic room without answering my question.

Chapter Ten

⁓⫶⁓

The only time it was less than impossible for my sister and me to get out of the house on our own was on Sunday mornings, when I told Janika we were going across town to church. Here was a request she could never refuse. Oddly, she and Joszef never went to Church, though she always bragged about being such a good Catholic. "Light a candle for me," Janika would always say when we left the house on Sunday mornings.

So, once a week, Heidi and I had a few hours when we weren't at the beck and call of the Feketes. Some Sundays we'd meet Béla at a café near his office but he was very busy with work and it was dangerous for us to travel too far from our new dwelling. Every day now there seemed to be more and more militia on the streets.

After spending most of the week indoors, I was content to find a park bench and sit in peace and quiet in the fresh air and sunlight. At first, Heidi joined me but after she met Andras, she began sneaking off by herself on those Sunday mornings. She was getting more and more bold, staying away for five or six hours at a time or slipping out to see Andras during the week when Joszef was with a client.

That was when she and I started to argue about Andras. Heidi was still so young and part of me understood that being in love was everything to her. Still, she was being reckless and I worried constantly that she'd get into trouble. Or, even worse, that she would get picked up, along with Andras. It was becoming just as dangerous to be around Jews as it was to be Jewish. I tried to stop Heidi from seeing her handsome vegetable man—I really did—but she would not listen to me.

"It's my life," Heidi told me more than once, "I'm old enough to do what I please. And you are not my mother!"

But I felt like her mother. I wanted to protect her as best I could. She was the only family I got to see now. My parents and my other siblings, Rose and Emil, were lost to me. It had been months since I'd seen them. Béla kept me updated and I knew they were in a safe house but nothing felt entirely "safe" anymore. I could not help but worry about the future of my family during those terrible days. Partly this was selfish, as I honestly did not know what I would do—or how I would survive—if anything happened to my loved ones, especially Heidi.

After one particularly bitter argument where Heidi accused me of being in love with Béla and denying her the same privilege with Andras, I decided to keep my opinions about her love affair to myself. So I bit my tongue and let her do what she needed to do. I prayed for guidance and for help but it never came because, suddenly, Heidi had been blindsided by life and, I suppose, by love.

Heidi's romance with Andras exploded into more tragedy than I ever anticipated or could possibly have imagined. What happened was so awful that it is still hard to talk about it, even

after all these years. I was not there to witness the events that
almost robbed my sister of her sanity and her will to live but
I learned about them soon enough. I wish I could keep this
part of our story a secret but I swore to tell everything that
happened and this was a big part of it and must be included.

Late one afternoon, on a gloomy day, Heidi returned early
from the office. This was unusual for her. I saw her walk
quickly into the house and heard her forcefully slam the front
door behind her. Janika yelled out—slamming of doors was
strictly forbidden in her house—but, without even calling out
a greeting, Heidi raced up the stairs to the attic. I was concerned
because she'd never before acted so rudely to Janika. No
matter how angry we ever got, we always made sure we never
showed it to others, especially the Feketes. I made some excuse
to Janika and quickly followed Heidi up the stairs.

When I entered our tiny attic room, I found Heidi sitting
on our bed. Her face was as pale as our bed sheets. She was
biting her lower lip so intently that it was bleeding. Her eyes
had gone completely glassy and she did not look up when I
entered the room. I could actually see that, beneath her coat,
her entire body was trembling. Her hands felt ice cold when I
touched her and she recoiled from me. I thought she might be
in shock so I wrapped a blanket around her shoulders.

Her arms were folded over her chest and her purse was
locked inside her forearms. I tried to pry the purse from her
clutches but she was holding on as if her life depended on that
purse.

I asked her what had happened. Was she sick? Did she need

a doctor? But she just shook her head from side to side and said nothing.

It took me a long time to coax her into lying down. I removed her shoes and finally convinced her to let go of her purse. She would not let me remove her coat. Even with the blanket around her shoulders, she continued to shiver. I could hear her teeth rattling together, even though it was quite warm in the attic.

She would only say four words: "Just leave me alone."

From downstairs, I heard the front door close, which could only mean that Joszef was home. Janika always wanted them to sit down to dinner the moment Joszef came through the door so I knew I did not have much time with my sister. I implored her to tell me what was had happened but she would not even look in my direction.

A few moments later, Janika called out my name from downstairs and ordered me to put dinner on the table. I wanted to scream back at her to just do it herself but, of course, I dared not. I didn't want to leave my sister but I had no choice.

"Darling, I have to go," I told Heidi. "Will you be all right?"

Heidi waved a hand and nodded her head just once. She wanted me to go. Despite my better judgment, I had to leave her. Racing down the stairs, I cursed the God who had created such havoc in our lives.

I served dinner as quickly as possible, my mind never far away from thoughts of my sister. Throughout dinner, whenever I came into the dining room, Joszef would steal glances at me from the corner of his eye. He seemed oddly more cheerful than his usual morose self. He even raised his head from his newspaper once or twice to speak to his wife, or at least pretend he was listening to her.

Of course, I could not ask Joszef if anything had happened

in the office that day. Janika had forbidden me from talking while I was serving dinner. She even insisted on ringing a small bell when she wanted me to clear to dishes instead of calling out my name. I think she really enjoyed the concept of being waited on by servants. That night she was thrilled with her husband's ersatz attention that she didn't seem to notice my sister was not eating her dinner in the kitchen with me, as she usually did.

It felt to me as if dinner lasted for several hours as Janika lingered over her coffee and tried to engage Joszef in a conversation about baby names. But then, finally, the meal was done, Joszef was in his study, the dishes were washed and Janika dismissed me for the evening.

I made a cup of tea and buttered some bread for Heidi, then raced upstairs only to find my sister in the exact same position as when I left her. I don't think she had moved one inch. She refused to eat and the tea went cold on the bedside table.

I spent the next two hours begging her to tell me what was wrong. By then I was crying in frustration. But Heidi just turned her head to the wall and closed her eyes. She would not look at me.

I splashed water on my face and changed into an old pair of pajamas Janika had given me. I did not try to undress my sister; she clearly did not want to be touched. I crawled into bed and lay down beside her. I closed my eyes and prayed for her.

Exhausted from the tension, frustration and worry of the day, I fell into a troubled sleep.

I was awakened sometime very early in the morning, hours before dawn, when Heidi turned in the bed and gave me a gentle nudge.

I felt her cold fingers on my shoulder but I was still groggy from sleep. She leaned in close to my head.

"He knows," Heidi whispered in my ear.

Cobwebs fluttered in my head and I tried to will myself awake. I didn't know what time it was or, for a moment, where I was. Then the memory of Heidi's face and demeanor that evening flashed in my mind and I remembered all of it. Even so, I had no idea what she meant. I rubbed my eyes.

I looked up and Heidi was leaning on one elbow and staring directly into my eyes with an urgency that was terrifying. "He knows," she repeated, this time with a kind of hissing sound to her voice.

"Okay, darling, it's okay," I said in my most soothing manner. I tried to sit up in bed and understand what was happening. I felt like I needed to be very careful now that she was actually speaking again. "First, tell me who you mean," I said, patting her hand.

"Joszef," she whispered.

"And what does Joszef know, darling?"

She leaned in even closer and cupped her hand around my ear. "He knows about us," she whispered hoarsely. "He knows we are not Maria and Eva. He knows we are Jews."

I jerked upright in bed as if an electrical charge had run through my spine. I could not have been more startled by Heidi's words. I stared into her frightened eyes and she nodded her head several times.

"But how? What? Heidi, my darling girl, what are you saying?"

She kept nodding while fat round tears began falling from her eyes. She opened her mouth but no words came out. And that is when she started crying in earnest. She was overcome with emotion and for a very long time, her body was wracked with sobs.

She was too hysterical to talk; I could see that. All I could do was try to keep her warm and protected until her nerves subsided and the thunderstorm of emotions passed. I don't know how long I lay in bed holding her and trying to muffle her cries. I was praying that the sounds of her hysteria could not be heard downstairs, though I was relatively certain that both the Feketes were sound asleep.

Once Heidi was a bit calmer I got a small, wet towel and placed it on her forehead. Then I tiptoed downstairs in my bare feet and quietly made my way to the liquor cabinet in the parlor. Though it was locked, I knew where Janika kept the key. I poured a big shot of brandy into a water glass and brought it back upstairs. This was an incredibly risky move, as Janika would've fired both of us on the spot if she'd seen me taking the liquor. But I didn't care. Heidi needed something to settle her nerves and later, after what she told me, so did I.

After taking a sip of the strong alcohol, Heidi managed to calm herself and tell me what had happened on that terrible day. Her story came out in dribs and drabs, somewhat incoherently so it took several hours until I really understood what had transpired.

Her day had started as it usually did. She had seen Andras on her way to the office but only briefly to nod hello and make a plan to meet that Sunday by the Protestant church near the Chain Bridge. Joszef was away that morning on some court business so Heidi was alone at her desk for several hours dealing with paperwork. Then, sometime around mid-morning, Joszef returned to the office with a Nazi officer. He introduced the officer to Heidi as SS-Obersturmführer Otto Skorzeny, a senior aide to Eichmann. This was a little unusual as Joszef rarely introduced his visitors to my sister.

And Skorzeny was no ordinary visitor. Heidi said he was one of the most evil looking men she had ever seen; she was immediately frightened of him. Short and rather squat, SS-Obersturmführer Otto Skorzeny had a long, ugly scar running from his chin across his left cheek and all the way to his ear. His thick black hair was oiled down slick and close to his scalp; his fingernails were buffed and polished. He was a highly decorated Nazi officer who wore a bunch of medals, a large handgun and a very ominous hunting knife in a leather pouch. Joszef made a point of telling Heidi that the Nazi officer was a close friend of Janika's father. "He was as fat as a pig," Heidi said, "and twice as mean—a horrid little man with a pig face. When he touched my hand, he made my skin crawl." A look of revulsion came onto her face when she spoke his name.

Skorzeny and Joszef spoke in private for about an hour, then the Nazi left the office.

That is when Joszef called Heidi into his private office. She brought along her pad and pencil, thinking he wanted to give her some dictation but, instead, Joszef closed the blinds to his office window. He walked over to the door and switched the "Open" sign to "Closed." Then he sat down on the small couch in his office and told Heidi to come sit next to him. This made her nervous but she did as she was told.

He took a bottle of whiskey from his desk drawer and offered her a drink and that is when she really became alarmed. She had to concentrate very hard to hide her fear from him. Joszef had never before offered her anything to drink or sat quite so close to her.

Heidi declined a drink but he took a long gulp of the

whiskey and said he'd had a very interesting conversation with Obersturmführer Skorzeny. Then he put his sweaty hand on her knee and said, "It seems as though there are no such people as Eva Varga or Maria Kovach from the village of Csenger. Skorzeny was very thorough in checking all of the records. You and Maria do not really exist so, as a law-abiding citizen, I think I have no other choice but to report you both as Jews living under false papers. And you know what will happen to you then." As he spoke, his hand traveled up her thigh.

Then he drank some more whiskey as he allowed Heidi to absorb that shocking information.

Heidi told me it took all her strength and fortitude not to faint right there on the floor of the office. She could feel the world spinning around her and bright lights sparking in the back of her brain. She was repulsed by his touch and considered getting up and running. "But where could I run to?" she asked me, helpless even in the retelling of her story.

That is when Joszef leaned over and unbuttoned Heidi's blouse.

She could not fight him off—she knew it and so did he. So she did not resist when he ripped off her undergarments and pushed her back on the couch. She wished then that she had fainted.

She told me she cried silent tears and bit her lip until it bled to stop herself from screaming through the ordeal, which was both revolting and painful to endure. Heidi had been a virgin up until that time and she had never imagined anything so brutal happening to her.

While telling me about this horrible experience, Heidi seemed to change all at once. Her lovely innocent face now wore a mask of sorrow and I noticed there were new lines in the corners of her mouth. It was as if she had aged ten years in the span of one day.

"I did what I had to do," she said, resigned and angry, "like you always told me we had to do."

I covered my face with my hands, a wave of guilt swept over me. Yes, I had told her that we had to do whatever was necessary to survive and I understood that some part of Heidi's rape was my fault.

Heidi did not want to give me any further details of what Joszef made her do in that stale, smoke-filled office and I was relieved because I did not think I could bear to hear any more about her ordeal. Overwhelmed, I suddenly became violently ill and, to my own regret and horror, vomited in the sink in our room. I wish I could've hidden my reaction but it was impossible. The thought of that horrible man raping my sister was far too disturbing.

And her story was not nearly done. There was much more—and much worse—to come.

After Joszef was done with Heidi on the couch, he told her to get dressed and he watched as she did.

Humiliated and bleeding, she did exactly as she was told.

When she was somewhat presentable, he said, "Come with me."

He had his cold, clammy hand on the back of her neck as they walked out of the office and stood in the doorway of the building. All that Heidi wanted at that moment was a hot bath and to be as far away from Jozsef as possible.

Across the street, Andras was sweeping in front of his vegetable stand. He looked up when he saw Heidi and smiled.

Seeing him made Heidi feel all the more humiliated and upset. "I couldn't look him in the eyes," she said. "He was only across the street but it felt like he was miles away. Now there was this huge abyss between us. If I told him what had just happened, could he ever forgive me?"

Just then a military transport truck came roaring down the street and stopped across from Jozsef's building. Two soldiers jumped out of the truck and ran towards Andras and his vegetable stand. They stood on either side of him.

Andras dropped his broom to the ground and stood there defiantly. He looked calm and steady. "He was unafraid," Heidi said, proudly. "There was no fear in him."

SS-Obersturmführer Skorzeny emerged from the cab of the truck and the sight of his ugly pig face made Heidi gasp. Skorzeny headed straight towards Andras who stood at his vegetable stand with his hands planted firmly on his hips but his eyes focused on my sister.

Heidi tried to call out to him. "I wanted to tell him to take off that horrible yellow star, I thought that would protect him," she sobbed as she told me what happened. She even started to cross the street but Joszef gripped her arm tightly and told her not to move.

I could see the deep red welts on her arm from Jozsef's fingers.

Heidi called out his name but Andras held up his hand to stop her. "I am not afraid, my love," he called out to her.

This seemed to enrage Joszef even more. He waved at Skorzeny and pointed towards Andras.

Skorzeny removed the Luger from his holster and shot Andras in the head, opening up a huge hole where his face had been.

As blood spurted out from his wound, Andras fell into

a heap on the cobblestones. His body laid twitching and convulsing for a few moments before going completely still.

Skorzeny returned the Luger to his holster and signaled to the two soldiers. He barked out an order.

Before Heidi could even grasp what had just happened, the two soldiers lifted Andras and carried his lifeless body to the truck. Then they tossed him inside the vehicle.

Heidi felt her knees give way under her but Joszef held her in a standing position and walked her across the street. She tripped once but he kept pulling her until they were standing next to Skorzeny.

Heidi could smell the burning scent of gunfire.

Jozsef extracted a wad of bills from his pocket and handed them to Skorzeny, who nodded and walked back to the cab of the truck.

Joszef and Heidi stood there by the vegetable stand as the engine of the truck turned over and the vehicle moved down the street and out of view.

Heidi looked down in disbelief at the blood flowing between the cracks on the cobblestones.

Chapter Eleven

⚜

What can you say to someone who has just witnessed the execution of her lover? I was, of course, shocked, saddened and outraged by the death of Andras but, God forgive me, I was more concerned about the safety of my sister. Andras was gone; there was nothing I could do about that. But Heidi and I were still alive and I had to think quickly about what was best for our survival.

My brain was in a whirlwind. I did not know what to say so I said, probably, the worst possible thing I could say. "It can't be true. I don't believe it."

Heidi looked up at me. "Are you calling me a liar? So now I am liar as well as a whore?"

I began pacing across the floor of our small room, the anger rising inside me. I lashed out at Heidi, even though she was the last person in the world I wanted to hurt. "How could you let this happen?" I said to her, blinded by frustration and rage. "I told you that seeing Andras was dangerous. Why couldn't you listen for once in your life? Do you have any idea what you've done? If Janika finds out about you and Joszef, she'll…"

Heidi threw her pillow across the room. "I had no choice, Gizi," she shouted back at me. "What did you expect me to do? If I'd refused him, he would've turned us both in. And that Nazi pig would've shot me too. Would you rather that I was lying in the street with a bullet in my head? Don't you understand? It wasn't my fault!"

She was getting hysterical again so I threw my arms around her and held her tight.

"We do what we must," she said between sobs, "that's what you told me and that's what I did. But what does it matter now? Without Andras, I am nothing. I might as well have died with him."

The alarm clock chimed just at that moment. It was 6:00 A.M., time for us to get up, even though we had not slept all night. Janika would expect me to have completed my morning chores in the next hour so I had no time to talk any more with Heidi. I apologized to her, as best I could, for the things I'd said. I told her that everything would be all right; that she had indeed done the right thing; that we would talk later and that I had to hurry downstairs.

I splashed some cold water on my face and dressed quickly. I was bone weary and terribly anxious as I went downstairs, wondering how I would possibly make it through the day. By focusing on the death of Andras and Heidi's ordeal with Jozsef, I'd lost sight of the most important thing my sister told me.

"He knows!"

The thought made me stop dead in my tracks. My worst nightmare was now a reality. What would Joszef do to us now? What would he expect from Heidi? Even if he did not report us, what would happen if we had to leave the Fekete house? Where would we go?

I put the coffee pot on the stove and went outside to get

Joszef's morning paper. I threw the paper on the dining room table and it opened up. The headline proclaimed that the previous day the Allies had invaded Normandy and were moving east, pushing back the Germans. The date was June 7, 1944.

I considered this turn of events as I prepared breakfast. Surely the invasion was good news. Didn't this mean that the war would be over soon? I wished I understood more about politics.

It was difficult enough to try to understand what was happening in our own house. I tried to think calmly and rationally about our situation. What did it really mean that Joszef knew we were pretending to be Catholics? Didn't he have a huge stake in keeping our secret? If Janika found out about him and Heidi, there was no telling what she would do. Joszef's entire livelihood depended on being in the good graces of his influential father-in-law. One bad word from Janika's father could ruin Joszef and he knew it. For the next hour or so, I managed to calm myself with these thoughts. I told myself Heidi and I were safe and even tried to convince myself that the news of the invasion was an actual sign from God, meant only for me, to let me know that the war was almost over and that we would soon be safe.

[Looking back I can only be amazed at how desperate, naïve and, yes, foolish I was that morning to imagine something good could come from the horror of those days.]

Janika walked into the kitchen and handed me a list of the groceries she needed that morning. She was saying something about making sauerbraten that afternoon for dinner when the phone rang. She answered it and handed the receiver to me. "It's your Mr. Stollár on the line, Maria. Please tell him that, in the future, he should not call here so early."

I nodded and took the phone.

Without even a greeting, Béla said, "We must get to the train station, right now."

I smiled at Janika as if this was the most casual of conversations. "Béla, it's really quite early for a phone call," I said.

Janika nodded her approval at me and turned away.

"Gizi? Did you hear me?" Béla said, his voice even more urgent. "I am hanging up and getting my car now. I'll pick you up in 15 minutes. Meet me at the corner by the bakery."

"What has happened?" I asked, alarmed and concerned by the tone of Béla's voice.

"It's Emil and Imre, they've volunteered to join the German work force. No one can talk them out of this. You must talk some sense into them. You're the only one they'll listen to. I'll explain in the car. Go now!"

My heart was beating so rapidly in my chest that I could feel the throbbing in my ears. With a shaky hand, I returned the receiver to its cradle.

I ran into the kitchen and grabbed the grocery list from the kitchen table. I told Janika I'd get an early start to the day by going shopping immediately. At least I think that's what I said. Whatever it was, it was a good enough excuse because she just nodded and waved me out of the kitchen.

Heidi was coming down the stairs as I grabbed my purse from the closet. She had washed her face and combed her hair and, though her eyes were rimmed in red, she looked presentable enough. She gave me a quizzical look as I raced through the front door. I whispered to her that I would explain everything later but I was in a rush to meet Béla.

She shrugged at the news and continued walking into the kitchen.

It was a warm spring day outside; a blue bird was perched on the awning of the bakery. It always amazed me that the outside world could be so normal and calm, despite everything that was happening.

I stood on the street corner for a few minutes, nervously biting my fingernails until Béla drove up in his black car and stopped at the curb. I jumped into the car and we quickly took off in the direction of the train station.

"Béla, what on earth...."

He held up a hand to silence me. "Let me talk, I have a lot to explain and not much time. I went to see your family last night. I was able to bring them some food and we were just sitting down to dinner when Imre burst through the door."

"Imre?" I exclaimed. I could not imagine what he would be doing at my parent's apartment.

"Yes, his family is now living only a few blocks from your parents. Anyway, at first, your father thought Imre wanted to talk about you but Imre said he'd only come to say good-bye. He was leaving for Keleti Station and wanted your father to say good-bye to you for him."

"Why was he going to the train station?" I asked.

Béla raced through an intersection, narrowly missing a red trolley car. He cursed at the traffic before continuing. "Eichmann has called for volunteers to work in the German factories and Imre decided to go. He had some crazy idea that it would be better to work for a few months in a factory that to risk more deportations. I think he believed he could sacrifice himself for a few months of hard labor for the sake of others."

"Is that so crazy?"

"Gizi, it's insane! With the Americans pushing from the west and the Reds from the east, it's only a matter of time before the war is lost. The invasion this morning is the final nail on the coffin. But the Nazis are determined to achieve their final solution and if they become desperate, they'll kill every last Jew they can before they are defeated. But I could not convince Imre that this idea of self-sacrifice was sheer madness and then Emil decided to join him."

"Emil? But he's so young."

"Certainly young enough to believe these idiotic ideas about making a difference. Emil told your parents that being young and strong would only mean that he'd have no trouble surviving a few months working in the factory. Of course, your parents tried to dissuade him. Your father even forbid him to leave but he would not listen.

"Before they left, Imre asked me to tell you where he was going and to forgive him. I tried to stop them myself but couldn't. They would not listen to reason. Too many months of being cooped up in the ghetto and feeling helpless, I suppose. Anyway, your mother thinks you're the only person who can talk some sense into Emil. She said you are the only one he ever listened to and, since no one else could leave the ghetto, I said I'd call you first thing this morning and make sure I got you to the Keleti Station before the train took them away."

Béla took a deep breath as we pulled up to the train station. Groups of young men were crowding the streets, all heading towards the station. Apparently, Eichmann had managed to convince many of them to volunteer that morning. Béla parked his car and we hurried towards the station, scanning the crowd for my brother and former fiancé.

I held tight to Béla's hand as we made our way through the throngs of young men. I was confused and conflicted. It was so hard to sort out right from wrong when the world was so upside down. "Béla, maybe Emil and Imre should get out of

Budapest," I said over the din of the crowd. "Maybe they're right, maybe they do have something to prove."

"Like what, Gizi?" Béla asked, his voice raw with anger. He turned to stare at me. "What do they have to prove? You want Imre to prove to you he's really worthy of your love? And you want Emil to prove to the world he's really a man? It's utter madness. Don't be such a fool, Gizi. All they will prove is they can both die like anyone else."

Chapter Twelve

Béla's words cut like a knife through my heart. I may not have understood very much about politics but I trusted that he did. All doubts flew out of my head. I believed Béla when he said Emil and Imre were about to embark on a suicide mission and vowed to do everything in my power to stop them.

The train station was even more crowded and chaotic than the surrounding streets. The platforms were jammed with men of different ages—some quite young and others who were older than my father. Almost all of them had yellow Stars of David sewn onto their overcoats. There was a lot of shoving and jostling for position. How could these men be so eager to get on that train?

Family members and other loved ones surrounded a few of the men; others were alone and looked entirely lost and confused by their surroundings. Nazi soldiers tried to bring order to the long lines of men by barking out orders and pushing them into unwieldy lines.

There were a lot of Nazi officers at the station, more than I'd ever seen in one place before and the sight of them frightened me. For so long I had avoided any place where the soldiers congregated. I was always afraid that my "disguise" as a Christian woman would not work. Although I was not wearing a Star of David, I could still be swept up at any moment for no reason at all. I felt vulnerable and exposed so I grabbed Béla's warm hand for support. I dared not look into the eyes of any of the SS guards. I kept my head down and tried to look as inconspicuous as possible while I scanned the faces of the young men. Béla gently squeezed my hand, which provided some reassurance.

After several long and tense minutes, I spotted Imre near one of the trains. Actually, I first noticed his mother, who was gripping Imre's arm and clinging tightly to him. He was patting her shoulder, obviously trying to comfort her.

I quickly passed a group of Nazi guards and headed towards my former fiancé. As I got closer, I noticed that Emil was standing directly behind Imre's mother.

"Emil!!" I called out and started to run.

He quickly turned when he saw me. "Gizi!" he cried. "What are you doing here?" He smiled and opened his arms.

I rushed into his arms and held him tightly to me. "You must leave here at once," I said into his ear. "You must come home with us. Mama and Papa need you, so do I. Please don't do this, Emil."

It was clearly the wrong thing to say. Emil pushed me out of his embrace. "What the…? Did Papa send you? And you too, Béla?" He shook his head in disgust. "I've made up my mind. I'm sorry but I am going and that's the end of it. I'm a grown man now, Gizi!"

"No, you are not a grown man," I yelled back in frustration. "You are just a foolish boy with some grandiose ideas. You don't know what you are doing. Only an idiot would believe the Germans."

"And you are always right about everything, aren't you, Gizi?" Emil spat in anger at me. "Well, I'm done doing what everyone else wants me to do. I am going to Germany for three months and when I get back, you'll see that this was the right thing to do."

Imre put his arm around my shoulder and said, "Gizella, I tried to tell him to stay here with his family but he is very determined."

I recoiled from Imre's touch. "Like you tried to help me?" I spat out at Imre, still angry and upset at the way he had abandoned me when I needed him the most.

Imre's mother heard my words and pointed a finger at me. "My son is brave to volunteer," she said. "What does someone like you know about such noble acts of courage?"

I tried to ignore her.

"Imre, I know you are brave," I said, willing myself to keep calm. It went through my head that if I could talk Imre into staying in Budapest, perhaps my brother would do the same. "You don't have to prove anything to me or to anyone else. And you certainly don't need to get yourself killed for some stupid pride."

A young Jewish boy—no more than twelve or thirteen years old—stood craning his neck to hear what I was saying to Imre. He wore a blue cap and a matching scarf that had been hand knit, no doubt, by his mother. The boy moved closer to me as I spoke to Imre. He seemed startled by my words.

Before I could say anything more, Imre's mother stepped between her son and me. "Killed! What are you talking about?" she screeched, waving her arms. "He's going to work in a German factory where it's safer than here in Budapest."

The young boy in the blue scarf looked from her to me with anxiety in his dark eyes.

"Is it?" Béla responded. He put one hand on Imre's arm and the other on Emil. "Listen to Gizi, both of you."

"With all due respect Mr. Stollár, this is none of your business," Imre said. "We are only doing what needs to be done for our people."

"Yeah," Emil added. "By volunteering we are stopping the Nazis from ordering more deportations."

"You think you can stop the Nazis?" I asked, dumbfounded.

Béla shook his head. "How many men before you have already left on this train?" he asked gently but with emphasis. "How many of them have come back? You know how many? None!"

Tears welled up in my eyes. "Please listen to us, Emil. You must not get on that train. If you do, we'll never see you again."

Imre's mother screamed. "You are a filthy little liar! You were never good enough for my son and now you are proving it to all of us!" She raised her hand to slap me in the face.

Imre grabbed his mother's wrist mid-air. "Enough! I will not allow you speak like that to Gizi!" He turned her around and gently pushed her towards the entrance of the station. "Go home now, mother, I mean it. Get out of here."

Imre's mother burst into tears, turned and ran from us. Imre started to say something but before the words came out of his mouth, the boy in the blue hat and scarf screamed—a long horrible wail that sounded like the desperate cry of a wounded animal. He turned away from us and sprinted towards the entrance to the station. He was running as fast as he could; he was running as if his life depended on it—and it did.

An SS soldier yelled at him to stop but the boy continued running, picking up some speed as he neared the entrance.

The soldier shouted again, then raised his rifle, took aim and shot.

The sound of the gunshot startled everyone within earshot. Several men threw themselves down on the ground while others ducked behind garbage cans or anything other structure offering protection.

The bullet entered the boy's body just between his shoulder blades and the force of the impact raised him in the air as if he was about to soar gracefully over the tracks. He sailed through the air for just a moment and dropped with a thud, face down on the train tracks. His scrawny body shuddered as the life went out of him.

There was a moment of stunned silence in the train station, and pandemonium broke out. The men in line who had witnessed the brutal slaying all appeared to panic at once, which caused a commotion among those at the other end of the station who did not know what had just happened. The men and boys broke ranks from the long line and tried to run from the station, but the SS soldiers swooped down and herded them onto the train with the butt ends of their rifles. More soldiers—both SS and Arrow Cross—stormed in from the entrance in a virtual sea of uniforms and guns. There was a lot of yelling and screaming as family members tried to pull their loved ones from the lines. More shots rang out, which only made everyone panic even more.

Emil and Imre were being swept into the crowd that was being forced onto the trains. I screamed at them to run—*RUN FOR YOUR LIVES!!!*—but it was too late. They were pushed onto the train with the others.

I tried to reach out for my brother but there was so much shoving and shouting I lost sight of him. Then I felt my knees buckle as someone behind me fell forwards. I started to lose my balance and feared I would fall and be trampled by the mob. Just then, from behind me, Béla shoved his hands into my armpits and pulled me back up into a standing position. I quickly regained my balance and was back standing on my own two feet. With Béla behind me, we started moving away from the train.

Before we reached the entrance to the station, an SS officer stopped us. He looked me over from head to foot, jerked his rifle towards my face and ordered me to get on the train.

I was too stunned to speak. My brain felt frozen and I could not move my limbs. Béla came between the soldier and myself and angrily pushed the rifle away. "We're Christians, you bastard!" Béla shouted as he jostled me past. By some miracle, the soldier retreated into the crowd as Béla shielded me with his body. Slowly, we made our way through the mob of people as the train began pulling away from the station.

I turned to look back.

I could see Emil's face framed by one of the windows in the train. He looked so young and so scared. His eyes were wide with terror. It occurred to me that all we had done was frighten him. Emil tried to raise to wave but other faces crowded him out of the small window. His head bobbed up once and then was lost among the others.

Back in the car, I could barely breath. Would I ever again see my brother? Or Imre?

I felt a pressure in my chest as if my lungs were being pressed together. I tried to inhale but could not seem to take in any air. For several minutes I thought I was having a heart attack. I wasn't, of course, but looking back I think that my heart was certainly breaking into pieces. What happened to Emil and Imre has haunted me ever since that morning. I've spent a million restless nights reimagining that brief conversation in the train station. Sometimes I think I finally discover the magical combination of words that convinces Emil and Imre to not get on the train. In my dreams I manage to save them— but only in my dreams.

Béla kept saying it wasn't my fault; that I had done everything that was possible to do. I listened to his words but I did not believe him.

I was to blame for it and for a lot more.

"I don't want you to help me anymore," I said to Béla.

He turned and looked at me with a look of surprise on his face. "Why not?" he asked.

"I don't know!" I cried. "Because Imre's gone, because my brother went with him for reasons I don't understand. It's all my fault. I made them go. Don't you see? I protected Emil all his life except when he needed me the most. I didn't love Imre. And they both left me. And you keep taking all these risks just to help me. If I lose you then I don't think I can survive."

"Gizella, please stop torturing yourself," Béla pleaded with me, his voice raw with emotion. "You did what you could. We are all doing what we can. Please believe me when I tell you that none of what happened is your fault."

"No? Who else could be to blame? Maria? Certainly not Maria, she watches it all from the sidelines and tells herself this is what she has to do to survive. She remains silent and invisible. Silent! With the world crumbling around her, Maria does nothing, nothing to help anyone but herself. How did I ever become such a person? I am nothing but a coward."

Béla didn't respond to my outburst. How could he? He

tried to comfort me by patting my knee and reminding me that I was not to blame while I cried into my handkerchief.

After awhile, I wiped my eyes and straightened myself in the seat of the car. It was at that moment I decided I'd shed enough tears. I was sick to death of being so helpless. It was time for me to actually do something. Perhaps Béla was right. Perhaps I could not have prevented my brother or Imre from leaving Budapest but certainly there were things I could do. Remaining silent and pretending to be someone else did not seem like enough.

"I can't go on this way anymore," I said to Béla, twisting the handkerchief in my hand and shaking my head from side to side. "I can't keep pretending to be someone I don't even know. Why am I living like this?"

"To survive, Gizi. That's a lot."

"I tell that to Heidi every day but you do more than just survive. I know about your 'friends' and how you are helping others with fake passports and who knows what else. I want to be part of it, Béla. I need to do more."

"Gizi, that's impossible."

"But why? I am a capable person. I have skills to offer. There must be something I can contribute."

"It's not that! Of course you are capable. Look, I know this is hard for you and I know how much you want to help but the truth is that I promised your father I would not involve you in anything dangerous."

I was shocked to learn that my father had extracted such a promise from Béla. Shocked and a little insulted. Did Béla think I was still a child? Did he think I couldn't speak for myself?

"It's not that you can't think for yourself," Béla said, as if he was reading my mind. "But you must survive this war. You must live a long life for all the people who can't. On this, your father and I agree."

I tried to argue with Béla but it was like hitting my head against a brick wall. No matter what I said, he simply refused to change his mind. Béla had made a promise to my father. "A promise is a sacred thing," Béla said. "I gave your father my word. Please don't ask me to betray his trust."

I gave up talking to him and turned my face to the window. We sat in silence for several miles.

Before dropping me at the Feketes, Béla wanted to stop and tell my parents what had happened. He knew that they needed to know.

The car pulled up to the ghetto where my parents were now forced to live. I stared at the wooden gates and the yellow Star of David painted across the wooden boards.

"I'll just be minute," Béla said. "This is not the kind of news they should hear from a stranger. I'll tell your parents about Emil, then drive you back to the house. Wait here, I'll be right back."

I put my hand on his shoulder to stop him. "No," I said. "I will do it. Give me your press pass."

Béla started to protest. He raised his hand as if to stop me. "You can't get past the guard at the gate, Gizi. It's too dangerous."

"It's just as dangerous for you," I pointed out. "Béla, listen to me. This isn't about me wanting to do something risky just for the hell of it. This is my family and it's my place to tell them about Emil. It will be better coming from me. I can do this. Don't be afraid for me and, please, don't argue, I couldn't stand it. Just give me your pass. I will be back shortly."

Béla exhaled slowly. Then he reached into his coat pocket

and slowly removed a small leather wallet that contained his pass. Resigned, he handed it to me.

I held the pass in my hand as I opened the car door and walked towards the ghetto.

An Arrow Cross guard stood at the gate. He was young— younger than Emil I guessed. He was smoking a cigarette in one hand while the other hand rested on his holster. He watched me intently as I approached him. His lips parted in a kind of sneer and his hand hovered over the Luger nestled in his holster.

Undaunted, I kept on walking. I was no longer going to be afraid. My only brother had just been carted off to certain death; my sister had been raped. I was not going to let them do anything more to my family. If this bastard wanted to shoot me, then let him do it and get it over with. He could not intimidate me.

As I got close to the gate, I flipped open the leather wallet and flashed the ID at the guard but not long enough for him to get a good look. "Member of the press, on assignment," I said in my best and most formal German.

I kept walking at a brisk pace before he could protest.

I was through the gate in a moment.

My heart was beating wildly as I climbed the stairs to the second floor. I stood outside the door to my parent's apartment for a moment to get my bearings. Part of me was thrilled to know my family was on the other side of this door but another part of me was devastated by the news I had for them.

I asked God for the strength I would need and rested my head on the door for a moment. I took a deep breath before I knocked.

My father opened the door and I fell into his arms, momentarily relieved and comforted by his familiar embrace.

Chapter Thirteen

Several weeks went by without any word from Emil or Imre. I suppose it was foolish to think we would hear from either of them but I tried hard to remain positive and hopeful, even though the two emotions were in short supply during those days.

Outside Hungary, the war continued to rage. I became much more attentive to current events, hanging on every radio newscast and reading every newspaper Joszef brought into the house.

The Allies were rampaging through Occupied Europe, beating back the German army. Soviet tanks rolled through the bombed out rubble of Vilna, Poland. General Bradley's American forces broke through the German lines at Saint–Lo in France. Smoke rose from the city of Gdansk as Russian forces approached the Vistula River near the Baltic Sea. General Patton's western troops barreled through France, getting closer and closer to Paris. Raoul Wallenberg continued his work by getting 630 visas to the Jewish counsel. When Romania surrendered to the Allies, newspapers started editorializing that the Red Army could not be defeated.

In Budapest, the deportations had stopped. Several weeks had passed since the last round up of Jews. I began to hope that perhaps Emil had been correct; maybe the deportations were done and he would return in a few months. I started praying that Béla had been wrong all along about the volunteers who had left for Germany.

Inside the Fekete house, I was continuing my duties as usual but, for Heidi, things went from bad to worse. Joszef continued to terrorize my sister. He was demanding she have sex with him several times a week. Or maybe more. I'm sure she spared me many of the more sordid details. My poor darling sister was so brave and so stoic through it all. Somehow she endured in order to ensure our safety.

We both knew that at any moment Joszef could report us to the SS, though that would mean bringing down a lot of trouble on his own head. The SS would want to know why he kept us employed if he knew about our real identity. How would he respond to that? And if Janika ever discovered his indiscretion, she would've made more trouble for him than the Nazis.

Meanwhile, though Heidi said she was all right, she changed a lot. She never mentioned Andras after the awful night that he died and she never again talked about falling in love. Her girlhood passion for romance novels vanished, as had the animation in her demeanor. Her face became something like a mask and she rarely displayed more than one expression, showing neither despair nor happiness. I knew that she was suffering terribly even though she did not share her feelings with me. I thought it best not to pressure her into telling me anything that was painful for her. She kept her secrets locked tightly in her heart and never revealed her anguish to me or to anyone else, as far as I knew.

Every once in a while, however, her bitterness would erupt, and I never knew what would set her off.

One day, for example, we were waiting in line at the bakery to buy some bread. The sign above the shop read: "Jews Only Allowed between 11:00 and 1:00." I sighed. This was not at all unusual and although I had been seeing these signs for months now, I was still upset by them. It broke my heart when I'd see a line of Jewish women, four or five deep, all straining to buy food before they were denied the privilege. Whenever possible, I bought extra food and delivered it to the ghetto. I no longer worried about Janika counting my change. I'd steal coins from her purse whenever I could. And my salary, meager as it was, all went to buy food for the Jews. It was little enough to do, I knew that, but it made me feel better to know I was doing something.

That day, I had a huge bouquet of purple and white flowers in my arms that I'd just purchased for Janika. There was some change left over from the florist, which I was using to buy bread.

The shelves in the bakery were almost bare by the time we made it to the top of the line. I handed the flowers to Heidi to hold for me as I approached the baker and asked if it was possible to buy more than one loaf.

"You know the rules," said the chubby baker, sweat pouring from his brow. "One to each family while rationing is going on."

"But just this once," I pleaded with him. "Maybe you could allow an exception. I'll pay you extra."

The baker stood on his tiptoes to look me over from behind his counter. "Why do you need more?" he asked. "You're not thinking of giving bread to those dirty shysters, are you?" He wagged a crooked finger at me.

"What!?" I asked, stunned that he'd guessed my exact intentions but knowing it was crucial for me to appear indignant at the suggestion. "No, no, I wouldn't give a bread crumb to a Jew." I slapped a disgusted expression on my face to emphasize my point. I wanted to spit on the hateful little man but I managed to refrain myself.

The baker laughed, seemingly pleased with my outburst. "That's more like it!" he exclaimed. "Look, I'd love to help you but those behind you might not appreciate my generosity."

He leaned over the counter and crooked his finger at me. As I leaned in towards his face, he whispered in my ear. "Come around back at closing and we will work something out, I'll save a loaf—and another big treat you will most certainly enjoy—if you return when my wife is gone." He gestured at a heavyset woman making sausages in the back room.

I took the one loaf he had in his hand, threw some change at the vile man and raced out of the store without waiting for Heidi.

On the street, Heidi ran to catch up with me. "What did he whisper to you?" she wanted to know as she handed the flowers back to me.

"That bastard wanted to trade certain favors for bread!"

"What kind of favors?" Heidi asked.

"Ones I am not willing to give," I responded.

She grabbed me by the wrist and twisted me around until my arm was aching. "Oh, but I am? Is that what you mean?" Heidi said, her voice shrill. "Why not ask me to go back and earn the bread for you?"

I shook free of Heidi's grip and started running down the street.

It took me several blocks before I had composed myself. I never knew what would trigger Heidi's temper and though I tried to be careful, being around her was like walking through a field of landmines.

I hurried back to the Feketes and as I unlocked the front door I tried to calm myself. It was always best to appear neutral and as low key as possible in their house.

Inside, the house was in a state of chaos as several hired hands worked furiously to get the rooms cleaned, the silver polished and the tables decorated for a party that night. More than forty top-level SS and Arrow Cross officers and government officials were expected for Janika's gala event and for weeks we had been busy making preparations. I had baked several cakes and three black market roast beefs were basting in the oven. In the kitchen, every surface was covered with enough food to feed a small army. It had been a very long time since I'd seen so much food in one place. Janika's influential father was the one most responsible for providing his daughter with such bounty. When I thought about the starving Jews who were begging on the streets for a crust of bread, this incredible spread of food made me as angry as a hornet. Already I was planning ways I could steal some of the meat and vegetables for those people who so desperately needed it.

I dropped the flowers on the kitchen table and took a deep breath.

Janika waddled into the kitchen just then. By now her belly was enormous and her chin had become encased in three rolls of fat. Though her doctor assured her she would only deliver one baby, she looked big enough to be carrying triplets. She had gained so much weight during her pregnancy that her entire body seemed to sway back and forth when she moved.

As if she wasn't mean-spirited enough, the extra weight made her cranky and irritated almost all the time.

Today, however, she was happy and excited about the upcoming party, "the social event of the season," as she called it—as if there actually were seasons for entertaining during those years. As I had anticipated, she forgot to ask me for the change from the flower shop so I pocketed the coins for future use. It gave me a secret little thrill to know that Janika's spare change would go to help feed the Jews she so hated.

"Help me arrange these flowers, Maria," she said with a cheerful lilt to her voice. "Get me that blue vase from the dining room and fill it with water."

"Certainly Mrs. Fekete," I responded and turned to leave.

"You can hold off calling me Mrs. Fekete until the guests arrive," she laughed. "Oh, and I got you and Eva two maid's uniforms to wear tonight. Please make sure they are starched and ironed. We have to impress our courageous SS officers!"

Later that afternoon, Heidi and I unpacked our uniforms from a box that Janika had left on the bottom of the staircase. They were short black dresses with lacy aprons and a silly little white triangle of a hat. We felt ridiculous wearing those costumes but of course we could not complain.

The guests started arriving around five o'clock. The men wore formal tuxedos or well pressed uniforms decorated with medals and ribbons. The women were dressed in satin and silk, dripping with furs and jewels. Most of them were heavily perfumed, with elaborate hairdos and many layers of make-up. It had been so long since I'd seen people dressed up that it was kind of shocking to me. I kept thinking of those poor Jews behind the gates in their tattered threadbare coats, decorated only with yellow Jewish stars. The world seemed so out of proportion and so completely senseless that I could not believe the earth was still spinning on its proper axis.

Heidi and I were told to pass around trays of delicate hors d'oeuvres—Russian caviar and puff pastries filled with smoked salmon—and fill drink requests for the guests, who huddled in small groups. The air became heavy and dense with smoke from cigarettes and cigars. A Victrola on the mantel played soft music to accompany the gentle hum of conversation.

I was emptying an ashtray when I looked up to see Béla Stollár walk into the living room. He was wearing a black suit and a white striped shirt that seemed a bit too large for his lean frame. He was a head taller than any other guest and, even though his thick and curly hair was in desperate need of a cut, he was still the handsomest man in the house. He grinned when he saw me across the room.

I had not seen Béla since that day at the train station. I wasn't exactly avoiding him but I had come to think I was far too dependent on him and that it would be better if I kept some distance between us, both for his sake and mine. Being close to anyone seemed particular foolhardy, as well as dangerous.

Still, the look on his face and the expression in his eyes was so friendly and engaging that I could not help but smile back at him. He made his way across the room to stand by my side. "What are you doing here?" I asked, genuinely surprised to see him in the house. I touched the lapel of his jacket and then, embarrassed in case anyone had noticed me touching him, pretended I was dusting lint from his shoulder.

He touched my hand lightly. "Mrs. Fekete invited me. Didn't she tell you?"

I shook my head. "No, she didn't mention it," I said with a laugh. "We're not exactly best friends." Behind Béla I could see Janika looking at me and pursing her lips in obvious disapproval. "Please excuse me." I said, lowering my eyes. "I should go." I turned and quickly went back to the kitchen.

I took a silver tray from the counter and began filling it with assorted cheeses and olives. The kitchen door swung open and Béla stood silhouetted in the doorframe. His head nearly touched the top of the frame. "Is it safe to come in?" he asked. "Or are you still mad at me?"

"Oh no, I'm not angry with you Béla; it's just that…" I did not know how to explain all the complicated emotions I was feeling at that moment.

"No matter," he said, "I'll forgive you if you'll promise me this dance."

He took the tray from my hand and placed it back on the counter. Then he swept me up into his arms and waltzed me around the kitchen. He was humming in my ear and the feel of his breath on my neck made me giggle. For a moment I felt young again—but the moment passed quickly.

The kitchen door swung open and Heidi walked into the room carrying a tray of empty glasses. She stopped when she saw us and stood staring. We quickly broke apart and I went back to arranging my cheese tray.

"Heidi…I mean, Eva! How good to see you," Béla said and walked over to her. He leaned in to kiss her cheek but she turned her head away from him. He stood taller and, in a soft voice, added, "I am so sorry about your friend."

Heidi swept passed him, shaking her head as if to dismiss the remark. "No matter," she said with a shrug, as if she were totally indifferent. My heart lurched in my chest when I remembered her schoolgirl crush on Béla and how excited she used to be he when came to the house for dinner.

Béla looked at me with a quizzical expression on his face

but I just shrugged my shoulders. There was nothing I could say to him at that moment.

An awkward silence descended on the kitchen. Finally Béla said to me, "I need to speak with you later when you get a moment."

I smiled at him. "All right. Now go on, get back to the party. Enjoy some of that food. You are still too skinny!"

He waved as he left the kitchen.

I walked over to Heidi, who stood at the sink staring blankly out the window. "He was only trying to help," I said to her but she would not look at me.

She cleared her throat. "Mr. Perepatits is asking for another martini," Heidi said. "Can you bring it to him while I get those appetizers from the oven?"

"Of course," I replied and poured another Martini from the cocktail shaker.

Later in the evening I was picking up dirty glasses and emptying ashtrays when I noticed Béla deep in conversation with Joszef, Janika and Gusztav Rigo, Janika's father. Rigo was a well-groomed man with a walrus mustache and a receding hairline. He smoked fat cigars and liked to blow smoke rings while he pontificated about his opinions. He was a powerful and influential man with personal access to the hierarchy in the Nazi party, so people always pretended to hang on his every word.

Tonight was no exception. As I walked by I heard him say, "He assures me that all is well despite Romania's surrender."

"I heard that Regent Horthy has halted all deportations," Béla said.

Janika waved a hand. "Why would he do something as idiotic as that?" she asked, rubbing her protruding belly.

Joszef shrugged. "Pressure from Parliament I would

imagine. They received a report from England, isn't that right Mr. Stollár?"

Béla nodded. "The Brits call it the Vrba-Wetzler report after two Jewish detainees who escaped from Auschwitz. Their eyewitness accounts are quite horrifying."

"Horthy is a coward," Janika sniffed. "He refuses to stand up for us."

Joszef ignored his wife's comment and spoke directly to his rotund father-in-law. "What does our man Szálasi make of this Jew report?"

Rigo cleared his throat and pointed his cigar at Béla. "The Arrow Cross position is that it's nothing but Jew propaganda by the British to get Horthy to come to the bargaining table."

"Why is this report, this Jew report at that, so important?" Janika wanted to know. "Why would anyone think that two Jews would be telling the truth? And what makes anyone think the Regent would even consider such a thing?"

"The report claims the Jews are not being deported to be used for labor," Joszef answered.

"That's ridiculous!" said Janika. "If not for labor, why would the Germans even want them? They hate the Jews even more than we do," she added with a laugh.

Joszef shrugged. "They say, my dear, that the Germans are marching the Jews into gas chambers and killing them by the thousands. Perhaps even the hundreds of thousands." His tone of voice was as nonchalant as if he were reporting the weather in Berlin. Jozsef lit a cigarette and blew a stream of smoke towards the ceiling.

My eyes followed the smoke to the ceiling and a darkness settled over my vision. Pops of light seemed to go off behind my sight and, after that, I don't remember much. I know I dropped the silver tray I was carrying because I remember the sound of glasses breaking and the heavy tray hitting the wooden floor. I looked down to see that the glass had cut through my thick stockings but it did not really register. *Perhaps even the hundreds of thousands.* Is that what Jozsef had actually said. Was that even possible?

Janika yelled at me. I could see her lips moving and she was pointing at me but I could not hear or comprehend what she was saying. It was as if I had fainted without actually falling down. I felt as if all the air in the room had been sucked out and there was only this empty vacuum of space. I could not breathe. The only thing left in my brain was the image of my brother Emil framed in the window of the train.

I sank to the floor and cut my knee on a piece of broken glass. I watched as my blood pooled on the wooden slats. It didn't hurt because I could not feel anything. Béla leaned over me and touched my back. He said something but it was as if I was under water and could not hear his words. He gently pulled me up and got me into a standing position. I looked around the room and momentarily forgot where I was. I remember wondering why everyone was so dressed up. A woman with bright red lips and platinum blonde hair was pointing at me and laughing as if I'd done something very amusing. I could see a trace of lipstick on her front tooth and that struck me as being very peculiar.

Janika strode over and stood so close to me I could see the two spots of rouge on her cheeks. Her enormous belly poked out and was almost touching me. "You idiot girl!" she hissed. "Look what you've done! Those are crystal glasses from my wedding set. They were made in Vienna!"

I shook my head as my memory came flooding back. "I'm so sorry, Mrs. Fekete," I managed to mutter. "Can I please be excused? I am not feeling well."

Béla put his arm around my shoulders and started to lead me back to the kitchen.

"You are too softhearted, Maria," Janika called out. "You should be glad that those dirty money chasers are finally getting what they deserve."

Faces of the guests came into view and passed me by. I could not focus on the people around me. Everything was blurred and rimmed in a dull light. I looked over to see a line of people standing around the dining room table, holding plates and waiting to be served. And I flashed on the image of Emil, with Imre and *perhaps even hundreds of thousands* of other Jews, lined up and waiting to be escorted into a gas chamber.

Chapter Fourteen

⁓⟋⁓

For the next few weeks, I went about my household chores and did whatever Janika asked. I was mostly silent, grieving and in mourning over the loss of Emil and Imre. I knew they were never coming back. In all probability, they were already dead. And, aside from the actual loss of loved ones, the most excruciating emotional part was that we would never know, for sure, what had happened to them. Like so many millions of others, Emil and Imre disappeared off the face of the earth without anyone knowing when or where, without a proper funeral, without anyone sitting Shiva. Even years later, long after the war had ended, we were never able to find out what had actually happened to either my brother or Imre. All we know is that they never returned.

Those weeks after the party were among the hardest of my life. Sadness and depression settled over me like a heavy blanket. I barely had the strength to climb the stairs at night to our attic bedroom. I realized that whatever happened from this point forward, life would never again be the way it was before the war. Up until that time, I had carried this fantasy in my head that if my family could just make it through to the end of the war, we could go back to life as usual. I'd been kept alive by the vision of us together again, laughing at the dinner table or sharing another Chanukah celebration. I knew that would never happen. Even if the war suddenly ended now, my family had been irrevocably changed and there was no going back. The past was dead and gone and, if we managed to survive, we would have to create a whole new life without our beloved Emil.

I desperately wanted to be the one to tell my parents what I had learned about Emil's situation. I wanted to be there to offer whatever consolation I could. But that was not to be. It had become even harder for anyone to get into the ghetto where my parents were living. Béla was able to get word to them about Emil. I could not allow myself to think about how the news affected them.

In late August, Janika gave birth to a healthy baby boy that she named Gusztav Rigo Fekete, after her father of course. The birth of a healthy baby is always a blessing but, whenever I looked at that baby or held him in my arms, I could not help but wonder if he would grow up to be like his parents and grandfather. A baby is of course innocent and pure but I was haunted by these thoughts.

Janika took to her bed to recover from giving birth. She hired a nurse to care for Gusztav and seemed happier than I'd ever seen her. Jozsef was delighted with his new son, so the mood in the house was much more cheerful than it had been before the birth. Preoccupied with her baby, Janika stayed in her bedroom most of the day, feeding the infant and complaining about the summer heat.

It was still humid by mid-September when Béla came to the house and asked me to go for a walk with him. Janika was about to take her afternoon nap, so she said I could leave the house for a few hours. She gave me a list of groceries to pick up on my way home.

Béla took my hand as we walked towards the Buda Palace. I could see that something was happening at the palace. A crowd of people had begun to form in the courtyard; reporters with press passes in their hats were among those moving through the crowd.

"What is going on, Béla? Why did you bring me here?" I asked.

"Wait and see," he said, with a grin on his face.

We strolled around the crowd for a few minutes. Béla greeted a few of the reporters.

Then the crowd suddenly went quiet and all eyes were focused on an upper balcony of the palace, where a slew of microphones were arranged. I looked up to see Regent Admiral Miklós Horthy walk out onto the balcony. He waved at the crowd and stepped up to the microphones.

Horthy was a large, impressive man who always wore a military uniform, complete with gold buttons, an assortment of medals and ribbons, and shiny gold epaulets. He wore a white cap and white gloves and looked every bit as regal in stature and appearance as I believe he wanted to look.

He had aged a great deal since I'd last seen him, more than a year ago. His face was now heavily lined and his hair had a lot more gray than I remember. His face had a grayish pallor and it was obvious that the strain of the past year had taken its toll on him. Still, he seemed to be the embodiment of our country—grave and solemn yet still sturdy and determined.

Cameras began flashing the moment he walked over to the numerous microphones spread across the balcony. He cleared his throat and nodded his head at the crowd.

His son stood next to him and Horthy glanced at him once before he began to speak.

"My countrymen!" Horthy declared in that booming voice, which always demanded respect. "This is a day we will always remember as one of humble acceptance. The time has come to put an end to our suffering."

I looked up at Béla, who nodded at me.

The crowd was totally engaged and it seemed as though everyone was leaning forward, hanging on every word. Expectation and anticipation hung in the air like a cloud of smoke.

"Today we put an end to our suffering," Horthy declared, his arms raised in triumph. "No more will our fathers and sons be fodder for this horrible war being waged across our country and across all of Europe. No more will we send them into the jaws of death for nothing!"

The crowd cheered and Horthy waited a moment for silence to return. "To that end," he continued, "I have denounced our alliance with Hitler and have signed an Armistice with the Soviet Union."

There was a long moment of stunned silence as the people absorbed these words. Then, the crowd erupted in raucous cheers, whistles and applause. Hats flew into the air and men grabbed each other in triumph. The entire courtyard seemed to rise up as one.

Béla picked me up and swung me around in a circle. He held me in the air and kissed me on the lips. I felt a surge of joy, a feeling that I had not experienced in the longest time. We kissed again and both of us began laughing.

A group of people started singing the national anthem and someone began marching through the crowd with the Hungarian flag. People touched their lips to the flag and kissed it. Others tore the flags of swastikas off the flagpoles and the walls of the palace.

Horthy disappeared back into the palace, his son on his heels.

"Oh Béla!" I shouted happily over the din of the noisy crowd, "let's go tell my family!"

He nodded and took my hand. We started towards the other side of the city.

I was filled with a warm feeling of happiness. Could it possibly be true? Could the war really be over for us?

Through the streets of Budapest, news of the armistice spread like wildfire. People came streaming out of their homes, shops and offices and congregated in groups on every street corner. There was cheering and singing and, of course, glasses of beer and alcohol were being raised in celebration. Music rang out and people were literally dancing in the streets.

But our joy was only momentary.

As we rounded the corner near one of the ghettos, Béla and I were stunned to see a gang of thugs drag a Jewish man and his teenage son out of their apartment building and onto the street. Using billy clubs and lead pipes, they beat the Jews with heavy blows and shouted loud Anti-Semitic chants.

Béla's face turned beet red with rage. He dropped my hand and raced over to help the victims. He grabbed the arm of the young thug who held a club over the head of the Jewish boy. The terrified boy looked up at Béla and wrenched himself free from the thug. He ran to his father, who lay on the ground.

Enraged, the thug then turned on Béla and swung the pipe at him. The pipe grazed his forehead and blood spurted out as a big welt formed. Béla punched the thug and wrestled the pipe from his hand.

An Arrow Cross officer ran over to Béla, drew a gun from

his holster, and held it to Béla's bleeding head. "Back off!" the officer screamed.

Béla released the thug and stepped away from the officer holding the gun. His face was still red with rage and blood dripped down the side of his head. He touched a finger lightly to his forehead and breathed heavily.

I hurried to Béla's side, concerned about his injury. He pushed me away so that he stood protectively in front of me, blocking my view of the Arrow Cross officer.

"What the HELL do you think you are doing?" Béla yelled.

I touched his forearm, trying to warn him to calm down. These were not the kind of men with whom it was safe to disagree, especially in a public place. They were the ones with the guns, the lead pipes and absolutely no moral sense of right and wrong.

Another Arrow Cross officer and two more thugs continued to beat the Jews as the officer kept his pistol pointed at Béla.

"We are cleansing our country of this Jewish scum," the officer scowled at Béla. "Why are you so interested?"

I handed my handkerchief to Béla and he took it. He dabbed the white cloth at his forehead. "Haven't you heard about the armistice?" Béla asked.

The Arrow Cross men laughed as they walked away from the beaten Jews, who lay sprawled in the street. "Oh, we heard," the officer said, "but apparently you are not aware of the counter proclamation."

"What are you talking about? We just heard Horthy say that he was signing an armistice this afternoon!"

The officer laughed as he backed away, still pointing his pistol at Béla. "Regent Horthy has abdicated his rule to Ferenc Szálasi, the head of the Arrow Cross. So now we are in charge."

I clutched at Béla's arm.

"From now on the Arrow Cross will decide the fate of the Jews," the officer declared before he turned and joined the group of thugs making their way down the street. He raised his gun and fired a shot into the air. "We'll get rid of those filthy bastards like Horthy should've done!"

With that the gang of thugs and soldiers disappeared around the corner, laughing and hooting.

Béla stared into my face as we tried our best to assist the injured Jews. We got them into standing positions. The young boy was not beaten as badly as his father, who, fortunately, was able to stand. They both thanked Béla for his help as they wobbled back to their apartment building.

"My family…" I said to Béla.

It was clear that he was thinking the same thing. He nodded and said, "We must hurry."

Racing through the city we could see that in what seemed like only a few minutes, Budapest went from celebration to chaos. The crowds of cheering people had disappeared, replaced by hoards of angry Arrow Cross soldiers and their followers. I don't know how this had happened, and happened so quickly, but I was there so I can attest that it did.

As Béla and I ran towards my parent's apartment, we could feel the panic and terror in the streets. Businesses and shops shuttered their windows as quickly as possible. Bands of roving thugs, some accompanied by the Arrow Cross and some out on their own, roamed through the streets, shouting obscenities and throwing rocks and bottles.

Arrow Cross soldiers pulled Jews from the streets or from their homes. The gates to several of the ghettos that we passed were smashed open. We could see mothers being torn away from their children, pulled by their hair into the streets where they were beaten and left for dead. Gunshots rang out. Bonfires were started on many street corners and furniture from Jewish homes and businesses was piled high on the raging flames.

It was as if the world had gone from joyful to completely insane in the blink of an eye.

It was dangerous for anyone to be out in the streets so Béla and I found an empty storefront and entered through the open door. The store had been looted and only a few broken bottles remained on the floor. Someone had started a fire in the middle of the room but we were able to smother it out with an old blanket. We sat down behind the counter and decided to wait out the worst of the riot. Clearly, we were safer indoors than trying to make it across town in all the chaos.

We clung to each other and said very little. There didn't seem to be anything to say.

After an hour or maybe more, as it was hard to judge time, we felt it was much quieter on the street and we should take our leave. Hiding in doorways and walking through the back alleys, Béla and I made our way to the ghetto where my parents were living. By then it was late afternoon and the city had calmed down. An eerie silence spread through the streets of Budapest. The smell of burning wood and gunshots hung in the air. We passed the body of an elderly man lying in the gutter. From his wounds, it was obvious that he had been beaten and shot. His clothes were torn and muddy and his eyes were wide open. In his hands, he clutched his fringed prayer shawl. Béla stopped to take the man's pulse, then shook his head to let me know that the poor soul was gone. We hurried away from the corpse.

In some ways, that day felt like the end of the world. I remember thinking that things could not get any worse but of course, I was wrong.

We rounded the corner to see a gendarme standing guard at the gate to the Magdolna ghetto. I was relieved that the gate was still standing. At least the ghetto had not been attacked that afternoon.

I hid in the shadows as Béla walked up to the guard and flashed his press pass at him.

"Go away," the guard said. "I can't let you in."

"I must speak with Rabbi David Kornfeld of the Jewish Counsel. I am here on official business," Béla said with authority.

"My orders are that all Jews must remain indoors until further notice," the gendarme replied, clutching his rifle.

"You don't understand, I must speak with him," Béla said with urgency. "I am under deadline and must get a quote from him. It is quite urgent!"

Inside the ghetto, a window opened and I could see an old man looking down at Béla.

The guard looked up at the old man framed in the window and pointed his rifle at him. The man quickly retreated and slammed the window shut. "Look, even if I could let you in, it would do no good," the guard said to Béla. "The Rabbi and his family are not here. They were picked up in the marketplace this morning, along with many other Jews from this ghetto."

I gasped and made a move to walk out of the shadows but Béla turned and motioned me to stay where I was.

"Where have they been taken?" Béla asked.

"The Glass House," said the guard. "Along with the rest of them."

My heart began beating wildly in my chest. I grabbed the brick wall behind me and took in a deep breath.

Béla turned and raced back over to my side.

"Oh, Béla, the Glass House!" I cried. Tears welled up in my eyes.

Everyone knew Eichmann had converted the old Weiss

glass factory by the waterfront into a warehouse for Jews who were being deported to Germany.

Chapter Fifteen

Béla insisted that I go home while he rushed off into the night. I did not know where he was going in such a hurry but I had complete faith he would do whatever he could for my parents.

I had no other choice but to follow his instructions and head back to the Fekete house. Being out on the streets was scary, even more so than usual that night, but I was not afraid. By now I had learned how to travel the streets of Budapest after dark and how to be inconspicuous. I always carried a dark scarf and gloves with me. I knew every back alley, shadowy alcove and other secret hiding place. I knew which trees around the Fekete neighborhood were wide enough to hide a person's shadow.

I was extra cautious the night of the riots and managed to get back to the house in less than an hour. My stories of the riots in the streets distracted Janika from asking too many questions about why I got caught in the midst of all the commotion. These days, the baby was a major diversion for Janika and she focused most of her attention on him instead of Heidi or me. As I told her about the broken windows and bonfires, she held tight to little Guzstav. Placing him gently in his crib, she commented on how Budapest would be so much safer once all the Jews were finally gone. "They can drag them away or shoot them in the streets for all I care," she said as she smoothed a blanket over her infant son, "just so long as they get rid of every last one of them!"

Very early the next morning I crept downstairs and placed a call to Béla. I managed to reach him at home. He had been out most of the night and had discovered out that my parents and my sister Rose were indeed at the Glass House. He had an appointment that morning with his contact at the Swiss embassy to see about getting the visas we would need to get them out of the deportation center and back to the safe house. Then we could work to speed up the process of moving the family to Switzerland.

I told Béla that Heidi and I wanted to go with him to the embassy to help plead our case. At first he insisted it would be best if he went alone but I explained that both my sister and I were far too anxious to sit home and do nothing. Perhaps there was something we could say to the Swiss officials to expedite the visas; certainly we felt compelled to try. I was so adamant that he finally relented.

But how were we going to get out of the house for the day? Heidi solved that problem by talking to Joszef. I don't know what she told him but she managed to get him to agree that she did not have to go into the office that day. She also got him to tell Janika that I had to accompany Heidi on some kind of office errand. (Heidi could be very persuasive when she wanted something and, by now, Joszef was so enamored with her that she could get what she wanted from him—except of course for the one thing she really wanted, which was for him to leave her alone. Still, having him wrapped around her little finger did prove to come in handy, especially that morning.)

We left the house at daybreak and walked to a café near Béla's office where we were supposed to meet him around 8:00 AM.

Budapest had settled down somewhat after the last night's rioting. As few people were brave enough to venture out, the streets were almost empty. Piles of smoldering wood gave off an acrid odor. Some shopkeepers and building owners were busy boarding up broken windows, and other people were making an attempt to clean up the streets by sweeping up the broken glass.

Though it was relatively quiet, there was an air of anxiety in the streets. Shades were drawn in almost all the windows and doors were locked shut. Bands of Arrow Cross thugs, some of them no more than teenagers, roamed the streets, confident in their new power. Heidi and I avoided them as we made our way to the café.

We sat down at an outdoor table and ordered cups of coffee as we waited for Béla. Eight o'clock came and went. By 9:00 we were more than a little anxious.

"Where is he?" Heidi kept asking.

I patted her hand, trying to be confident enough for both of us. "He'll be here, don't worry. He has to be cautious."

Heidi glanced down the street. "I just wish he'd hurry." She looked at two Arrow Cross soldiers who were drinking beer on a street corner across from the café. One of the thugs tossed a rock through the window of an abandoned townhouse.

"That murderous Szálasi bastard!" Heidi exclaimed with passion. "Look what he has unleashed on us!"

"Keep your voice down," I warned her, alarmed by her open

display of hostility. "If they hear that kind of talk, they'll drag us away. We need to be inconspicuous."

"Yes, you're right, of course," Heidi mumbled into her coffee cup.

I looked at my watch again. Béla was now almost two hours late and I was getting increasingly nervous. This was definitely not like him. Where in heaven's name was he?

Another band of thugs turned the corner onto the street where we were sitting. There were five of them and they looked like they'd been out all night. They had dirty faces and rumpled clothing. God only knows what kind of havoc they had wrought. The boys were snickering and pointing at us as one of the thugs, a kid of about fifteen, swaggered towards our table.

He was a young but rough looking hoodlum with slicked back blonde hair and a lit cigarette dangling from his mouth. He wore a heavy gold chain on his neck and several gold watches on his wrist, all of which I imagined he had stolen sometime during the night. His black leather jacket was several sizes too large for him. His narrow chest was puffed up with self-importance as he approached Heidi.

"What're you two charming ladies doing loitering out here on this spectacular morning? Don't you know it's not safe for you to be out on the street until we're done rounding up the Jew pigs from Budapest? We're going to cart them all off to the park and watch them burn to a crisp, aren't we boys?" His companions snorted their approval of this gruesome idea.

The despicable kid reached out a dirty hand and touched Heidi on the shoulder. "Come, sweetheart, let me walk you home where you'll be safe." He removed the cigarette from his mouth and flicked it into the street.

His fingernails were caked with grime and Heidi recoiled from his touch.

"Thank you for the offer," I said evenly, "but no thanks. We are waiting for a friend to meet us here. We'll be fine."

The thug shot a murderous glance my way. Suddenly he seemed much older than his teen years. "It's not a request, miss, it's an order!" he said with authority. His friends, standing behind him, snickered their approval.

I stood up, furious that this child would talk to us in such a manner. I wanted to slap him across the face but knew I needed to control my anger. It was obvious he was not going to back down in front of his friends. Now his pride was at stake so the situation was even more volatile. "Come on, Eva," I said to my sister, keeping my voice as unemotional as I possibly could. "We'll just see ourselves home." I reached out my hand to Heidi who stood and grabbed it. We turned to walk away but the brat stepped between us. He put out his hands and pushed Heidi and me apart with a sweeping gesture.

"Not so fast!" he declared. "*You* can go home by yourself," he said, pointing to me. He jerked a finger at my sister. "I'll escort her." He grabbed Heidi's elbow as he shoved me aside.

There was no way I would leave my sister alone with these thugs but before I could say anything Heidi held up a hand to stop me from protesting. "Just wait a moment my dear," Heidi said to me with a smile, "while I sort out the problem with this young man." She exuded confidence and charm as she took control of the situation.

I had no choice but to take a step back.

"That's better," the boy grinned. "Now, darling, let's take a look at your papers."

Heidi smiled warmly at him. What the hell was she thinking? My sister opened her purse and wrenched out her papers, along with a pencil and a small pad of paper. "Of course, young man, but first could you please tell me your name?" she asked sweetly. "And spell it out for me so I get it correctly. I want to be certain my boyfriend knows exactly who kept his girl waiting with these silly games." Heidi held the pencil to the pad and looked directly into the eyes of the young man.

The brat turned to glance at his friends, who had stopped snickering for a moment and were looking perplexed at this sudden turn of events. The young thug did not seem at all alarmed. He winked confidently at his companions as if he were truly enjoying the moment.

"M-a-t-y-a-s B-a-k-y," he said proudly and slowly spelled out each letter as Heidi wrote. He pointed a finger at her pad of paper. "You can also write down that I am an Arrow Cross Junior Squad Leader." He gave her a little salute and, with only a cursory glance, handed Heidi back her papers.

Heidi continued to write as if she were making notes about Matyas.

He laughed. "And Miss Eva, who might your big bad boyfriend be?"

Heidi took her papers from Matyas and put them, along with her pad and pencil back into her purse. "SS-Obersturmführer Otto Skorzeny," Heidi declared as she smartly snapped shut her purse. "Perhaps you've heard of him, Mr. Junior Squad Leader?" She crossed her arms over her chest and cocked her head at him.

The boy shook his head, the bravado fading from his face.

"No?" Heidi asked and shrugged. "Well, let's see if I can find someone whose name you do know. My darling Otto is Senior Aide to Colonel Adolph Eichmann. Oh, you've heard of Eichmann, I trust?"

The boy nodded and swallowed hard. The color had quickly

drained from his cheeks as the implication of what Heidi was saying sunk into his feeble brain. He took several small steps backwards to be closer to his pack of friends. They, in turn, also walked backwards—away from Matyas.

If the situation had not been so potentially dangerous, I might have found it amusing.

"Umm, yes, of course! Colonel Eichmann is a great man!" the boy nodded with enthusiasm, still retreating. "I'm sorry, miss, I meant no harm...Umm...we will just be on our way now. Come on, guys."

Heidi glared at the boys as, almost in unison, they turned and ran down the street. "I'll tell Otto you send your regards," Heidi shouted out, laughing.

I watched them go with a sense of marvel and appreciation for my quick-witted sister.

"Well done, Heidi!" I exclaimed, planting a kiss on her cheek.

Heidi shrugged as if it had been nothing at all. "Just a toy soldier full of himself," she commented, picking up her cup and sipping her coffee.

Despite her nonchalance, I could tell she was pleased with herself, as well she should be. Many miracles had happened to save us so far but this one had been due entirely to my sister's newly discovered confidence and bravery. She had been through so much and had suffered terribly but I realized that morning that her ordeal had made her stronger. I was very proud of Heidi that day.

A few minutes after the thugs had left us, Béla's car came round the corner and I breathed a sigh of relief.

Béla leaned out the window and told us to get in.

He looked worn and tired and I guessed that he had not slept much that night.

I asked if he was feeling okay and he nodded. "Yes, I'm fine," he said.

"Did you find our parents?" Heidi asked as the car drove down the street.

"Yes, they are safe for now," he said with a nod of his head. "But we have to hurry. There's a lot to accomplish and not much time."

There was so little traffic in the street that morning that we soon arrived at the Swiss embassy.

Béla parked the car across the street and we hurried up the massive stairway and into the lobby of the building.

The embassy was mobbed that morning with a mass of desperate people. Makeshift desks had been set up on the marble floor of the lobby. The clacking noise of typewriters reverberated off the hard stone surfaces. In front of each desk, long lines of Jews stood waiting to be processed. Most of them were holding papers or filling out lengthy forms. The mood was relatively subdued but an air of desperation hung over the huge space. Fear and anxiety were almost palpable, almost as disturbing as the cacophony of typewriters.

"I'm hoping your family will be here," Béla said as he glanced around the room. "I got a message to them late last night that their visas would be ready and they should get here very early to pick them up."

Béla, Heidi and I split up so that we could cover the room and search for my family more efficiently.

I was on the left side of the lobby when I spotted my father and my sister Rose. I raced over to them and hugged Rose and then my father. Heidi ran over and practically jumped into my father's arms. She had not seen him since that morning we were separated on the street. Tears of joy ran down their faces and they clung to each other.

"Thank God you are safe!" my father exclaimed, kissing Heidi on the forehead and smoothing back her long dark hair.

Once Heidi stopped hugging my father I got a closer look at his face. He seemed to have aged a great deal since I'd last seen him, the night we lost Emil. For the first time in my life, he looked to me like a very old man. His face was gray and he was slouched over. He had lost a great deal of weight, and his wool coat hung loosely from his shoulders. My father had always been a tower of strength but today he seemed frail and vulnerable. It broke my heart to see him so reduced from his former self.

It took me a moment to realize my mother was not with them. I asked my father where she had was.

His face sagged even more and a look of despair came into his eyes. He started to speak but then choked on his words. Tears spilled from his eyes, which shocked me because I had never before seen my father cry.

"They came in the middle of the night," my father sobbed, shaking his head in disbelief. "I tried to stop them, I really did, but there was nothing I could do. Nothing!"

Rose nodded sadly. "Last night, we were asleep on the floor of the Glass House. It was the middle of the night. Suddenly, the lights went on and the SS troops marched into the warehouse." Rose's bottom lip began to quiver but she fought hard to maintain her composure. Like my father, Rose was not given to showing her emotions, especially in a public place. "It was utter chaos. People were screaming and trying to hide under the tables." Rose blinked back her tears. "They only took the older women. They grabbed them off the floor and didn't even let them get dressed. Mother was dragged away without her shoes." Rose held up a pair of my mother's worn black shoes.

"I tried to stop them!" my father repeated. "I tried but they shoved me aside like a rag doll. It's all my fault!"

I put my arm around Rose's shoulder and hugged her. Then I took the shoes from her hand. "Where did they take them?" I asked.

"They put them on trucks and drove off," Rose said. "I think they were going to the train station."

Béla and I exchanged a quick glance. I could see concern in his eyes and I am sure he saw the same reaction in mine.

My father straightened himself and wiped away his tears. "We were here at 6:00 to get our visas and I was just waiting until you arrived. I should go to the synagogue," he said. "The Counsel may be able to help before trains pull out. Béla, what do you think?"

"I think this wasn't your fault," Béla said. "And I don't think the Counsel can do anything to help at this point. I am so sorry, David."

"Give me Mama's papers," I said to my father. He reached into his pocket and handed me the Swiss visa. "Béla, give me your car keys."

Béla tossed the keys to me.

I grabbed them mid-air and turned.

"Maria!" Béla called but I kept on running. "Maria, be careful!"

I did not turn to look back. There was no time.

I had to make it to the train station before my mother was lost to me forever.

I drove like a madwoman through the streets of Budapest. Béla's little car screeched with protest but I did not pay any attention. I went through several stop signs and almost ran into a motorcycle.

My mind was racing even faster than the car. I had to have a plan. A million ideas ran through my head until I finally settled on one that seemed the most likely to work. I said a quick prayer, begging God for the strength to save my mother.

About half a block from the train station, I left the car by the side of the road, raced down the street and up the steps.

The last time I had been inside this glass-domed train station was the night Emil and Imre were taken away. I shuddered at the thought of seeing my mother's face framed in the window of the train.

I tried not to think about that evening as I scanned the long lines of people for my mother. She was such a tiny little woman that I worried I would never find her among all these other people.

Though the station was mobbed with people and SS guards, the building was bizarrely quiet and organized. An SS officer was standing on a wooden box by the first platform with a clipboard. He was calling out names and ordering people onto various platforms. (The Germans were nothing if not organized!) Most of the Jews were seated around the platform on benches or on the floor while Arrow Cross soldiers and civilians carrying weapons milled about, keeping people seated in their places until they were called.

I turned around in a circle, scanning the entire area. In a few moments, I spotted my mother. She was sitting on a bench with many other women, most of them gray haired and elderly; a few of them looked quite ill. Most of the women on the bench were crying—some were hysterical—but not my mother. She looked calm and resigned and I could see that she was trying to comfort the woman sitting next to her. My mother had her arm around her seatmate and seemed to be patting the woman's hand while she spoke softly to her. I could just imagine the words of encouragement coming from my mother's lips.

My mother was the bravest woman I have ever known and, whenever I think about her now, even years later, I remember the serenity on her face that day. Even though she must have known she was facing an uncertain and probably fatal destination, she was still focused on helping others.

I took a deep breath and squared my shoulders, reminding myself that I needed to convey an air of authority if I was going to be successful.

My mother looked up and recognized me as I made my way through the crowd. Her mouth formed into a tight little circle of surprise.

I walked boldly towards the bench where she sat and bent over her. I put the shoes in her hand. "Don't speak," I whispered in her ear, "just put these on and stand up."

I think she was too surprised to protest. She had some trouble with her laces so I bent down to help her and put my hand on her elbow. She stood up.

"Come with me," I told her.

She nodded silently and we started walking towards the main entrance of the station.

We did not get very far. A man of about thirty, dressed in civilian clothes but carrying a rifle and acting like he ruled the station, held out an arm to stop us. "Where the hell do you think you're going with that old lady?" he demanded with a sneer.

Before I could answer, an SS officer walked up to us. "Is there a problem here?" the officer asked.

I cleared my throat. "The Swiss embassy has just issued immigration papers for this woman," I said, holding out the visa my father had given me. "I am here on behalf of the Swiss government and Ambassador Carl Lutz to escort Mrs. Kornfeld back to the embassy. She and her family are scheduled to leave for Switzerland in a few days. She was taken away by mistake last night."

I tried to stop my hands from shaking as the thug grabbed the visa from me and handed it to the SS officer. While the two of them inspected the papers, I bent over and ripped open the hem of my dress. Many weeks ago I had sewn my most valuable possession into the hem, just in case I needed it.

This was the exact emergency I had anticipated.

When the thug looked away, I smiled at the SS officer and put my hand on the visa. "If you look here, sir," I said, "you will see that this woman is protected by the Swiss government."

I held my hand over the visa and dropped Imre's diamond engagement ring on the papers. "Please sir, take a closer look. You will see that the papers are all in order."

The officer looked up at me, then turned his back on the thug. I could see that he was examining the ring. Satisfied, he turned around to face us and nodded his head. "Yes, your papers are all in order," the officer said. He folded the visa and handed it back to me, without the ring, of course.

"You may go," he said and nodded towards the main entrance. "But go quickly before I change my mind."

The officer pocketed Imre's ring and resumed his supervision of the long lines. The thug went over to an elderly Jew and began bullying him back into line.

Without a moment's hesitation, I grabbed Mama's elbow and we started towards the door.

My mother and I walked as quickly as her legs would allow. We did not speak. I think we were both in a kind of shocked suspension. I feared the SS officer or that dreadful thug would come running after us. But fortunately, we made it to the door without any further interruptions.

Another miracle had saved us.

I guided my mother towards Béla's car, opened the door and helped her get seated inside. I slammed the door and exhaled, which made me realize that I had been holding my breath for the longest time. I walked around the car and got in on the driver's side. I found the keys in the pocket of my coat and tried to put them into the ignition, but my hands were shaking and I couldn't do it. This made me bark out in laughter, which surprised me as much as it startled my mother.

My mother touched my arm and we looked at each other for a long, long moment. Her hazel eyes were wide open. Her pupils were dilated and so filled with different emotions that they were almost without expression. "Overwhelmed" is the only descriptive word that comes to mind.

She held out both of her hands and I took them into mine.

Mama's hands were cold and so impossibly tiny; it felt like they were composed of bones as brittle as a bird's and that if I squeezed too tightly, I would hear a sound like branches snapping underfoot. I leaned over and gently kissed each one, holding them to my cheek.

There were no words that we could say to each other at that moment but, in this blessed silence, we acknowledged what words could not.

So we held hands and bowed our heads, touching foreheads for a moment. But I became aware that we weren't exactly out of danger. It was hardly safe for two Jewish women to be sitting in a parked car with all those SS officers on patrol.

I shook out my hands, jingling the keys. My right hand was now much steadier, so I managed to start the ignition and put the car into gear. The gears made a grinding sound but the car responded when I stepped on the gas.

Slowly, I pulled out into traffic while my mother, in a soft but steady voice, recited the Lord's Prayer in flawless Hebrew, a language I had not heard spoken in such a long time that it brought tears to my eyes.

Chapter Sixteen

I had driven only a few blocks before it occurred to me that I did not know where to take my mother. I was not going to bring her back to the Glass House; that was, certain. My father and sister Rose now had visas so they could return to the Swiss safe house where they'd been living before they were dragged out of their home. But would they go back there?

I was debating where they might be when my mother—who I always believed could read my mind—said, "Take me to your father, Gizi. I need to see him as soon as possible. He probably thinks I am dead."

"Of course, Mama," I replied, "but I am not exactly sure where he could be right now."

She peered at me with a very familiar expression on her face. This was a look I had seen throughout my childhood and it said to me, "Oh please, I raised you to be smarter than that!"

She smiled at me and I smiled back.

Of course, there was only one place in the entire world that my father would go in his time of trouble or uncertainty—the Dohány Street synagogue.

Next to his family, my father loved that synagogue best in the world. For Papa, and for thousands of other Jews in Hungary, the twin-spired synagogue was a symbol of our religion and the power of our collective spirit. Built in the late 1850s, the temple boasted two onion-blub cupolas that rose high in the sky, topping the largest and grandest Jewish place of worship ever built in all of Europe. Inside, the synagogue could seat more than 3,000 visitors. It was a spectacular building and the spiritual center of Jewish life in Budapest. It was also where the Jewish Counsel met, and my father was always there to offer advice and to seek counsel when he himself felt troubled.

Of course my mother was right--there was only one place where my father would have gone in his hour of need.

We drove towards the Pest side of the city and parked about two blocks from the synagogue. I thought it best not to park too close and my mother assured me that she could walk the short distance.

It had started to rain but it was only a drizzle and looked like it would not last long.

I took off my coat and put it around my mother's shoulders. I held her tightly around the waist as we made our way down Dohány Street. The night air and the gentle rain seemed to revive her and, in no time, she was walking steady and strong. My mother had untold reserves of strength.

"We'll be inside soon, Mama, and we'll see Papa," I said, trying to distract her with my chatter. "Then we will see about getting you something warm to eat."

"*Baruch Hashem*," Mama said which meant "Thank God."

Even with the drizzling rain, the sun shone dimly and I could see the familiar spires in the near distance as we got closer.

The sight would have cheered me except that coming

towards us down the street was a rowdy bunch of young men, Arrow Cross thugs from the looks of them. They were excited, even rather agitated, as they clapped each other on the backs and shouted at each other. I could hear them saying things like, "We really got that limp dick Yid bastard!" and "One less Christ killer for the gas chamber!" The bastards laughed at these crude and hateful remarks.

I shivered in my thin dress and held my mother closer, trying to protect her from the sight and sound of those hate-filled boys. As they passed us by on the street, I squeezed Mama a bit tighter. We both tried not to look at them, hoping we would not draw their attention to us. Instead I focused my eyes on the synagogue, which appeared before me like a haven of sanctuary and sanity in this torn and broken city.

Mama and I had begun climbing the front steps to the temple when I was distracted by the sound of loud, pain-filled moaning. I looked around but did not see anyone on the stairs. Who was making that noise? Then I heard the sound again and it felt vaguely familiar to me though I didn't know why. I realized the moaning was coming from the side of the steps.

I told my mother to wait for me under the awning, out of the rain, while I went to find the source of the sounds. I walked over to the right side of the stairway and looked down.

In the space next to the steps, in a kind of gutter between the synagogue and the building next door, I saw a man lying on his back and moaning. I could not see his face very clearly as he was facing away from me. He was clutching his right arm and began coughing in an alarming, rasping manner. From the disheveled look of his clothes, it was apparent that he had been beaten and left to die right there at the synagogue.

I heard the man chanting, *"Hashem roei lo schsar..."* (The Lord is my shepherd, I shall not want...)"

"Who's there?" I called out to him. "Are you all right?"

He turned his face towards me and, in a ray of light through the rain, I realized to my horror that the injured, bleeding man in the gutter was my father.

A high-pitched scream escaped from my lips as I raced down the steps. "Papa! No, no, no. Papa, it can't be you. Please, God, it can't be him," I heard myself shout, a prayer that evaporated instantly in the chill, wet air.

I threw myself down by his side.

My father's body was bent in the most awkward position; one leg was at a sharp right angle to his torso and it was obvious that at least one of his arms was broken. His face was cut and swollen where he had been repeatedly punched. And perhaps most shocking of all, someone had taken a knife and slashed off my father's beard. I had never seen my father without his long gray beard, a symbol of his devotion to God.

I looked up and my mother was at my side and tears were streaming down her face.

I leaned over my father and put my arms underneath him. I tried to scoop him up in my arms but he protested. "No, no, Gizi, don't," he said through clenched teeth. "Something inside is broken. It hurts too much. Please, just let me rest." His torn and swollen face grimaced in pain.

"What happened, Papa? Who did this?"

But he could not respond. He shook his head from side to side as if my questions were too trivial for him to consider answering.

"Somebody help us!" I screamed into the night. I did not want to let go of my father. I felt helpless beyond words.

My mother had one hand on my father's cheek and was

wiping blood from his brow with her other hand. She just kept chanting his name, over and over, in a low voice.

My father reached out a scraped and bloody hand to my mother. *"Yihyeh beseder ishti,"* he said to her, which meant "Everything will be all right, my wife."

"Ani ohevet otcha, baali," she replied. "I love you, my husband."

I was frantic with fear. "Someone please help us! My father is hurt!" I shouted again.

But no one came to our rescue.

It started to rain a bit harder.

"What can I do, Papa?" I asked, frantically. "Please tell me there is something I can do for you."

"Don't worry my child," he replied, his voice suddenly calm. "God will have mercy." He lifted a hand to what was left of his beard and his hand dropped to the ground.

Now it was really raining and I tried as well as I could to cover my father with my body. But when I tried to touch him, he would groan in pain.

"Please hold on, Papa, help will be here soon!" I was crying so hard by then that my tears were mingled with the rain.

"I feel cold, my daughter," he whispered.

I could feel him fading away from us and from life. I felt that he was disappearing right in front of my eyes. It was as if the energy in his body was seeping out onto the ground and evaporating into the air.

"Papa, don't go! We need you, please stay with us." I pleaded with him even though I knew my words were useless against a force far greater than my own.

My father opened his eyes and stared at me. Then he grasped my arm in a vise-like grip. He seemed to regain some of his strength and he spoke quite forcefully to me. "Listen to me,

Gizi," he said, staring intently at me. "Do not rely on miracles. Do what you have to do." Then his face softened. "Peace be unto you........."

His eyes focused on my mother and the light in his pupils dimmed. His body shuddered and convulsed, then seemed to relax. A drop of blood trickled out from the side of his mouth. He took a long, raspy breath and exhaled.

He died in my arms.

I don't know how long I sat there in the rain holding my father. It seemed like hours but it also seemed like only moments.

I felt like I was in a kind of empty space. Time slowed down or maybe stopped all together. I couldn't hear anything other than the sound of the rain hitting the pavement. I felt neither cold nor wet, though I suppose I was both. I was beyond feeling, suspended someplace in time. I might have remained in that exact position forever if Béla and my two sisters had not arrived.

They rounded the corner in a great hurry, breathless and upset. They were climbing the steps and I could hear them talking but could not make out what they were saying.

My mother called out to them and they came storming down the steps and into the alley.

Heidi screamed, then clapped a hand to her mouth.

"Oh Papa!" Rose cried.

"Papa's gone," I said. "I couldn't do anything to help him!"

My mother bowed her head and prayed. My sisters began to cry and their sobs soon turned into long wails of anguish. Mama put one arm around each of my sisters and held them tight.

Béla walked over and knelt down before me. He put a hand on my shoulder. "I'm so sorry, Gizi," he said. "I should never have let your father come here alone. I just didn't realize how dangerous it was."

Béla forced me to let go of my father and pulled me to my feet. I was reluctant to stand. I wanted to stay kneeling over my father as long as possible. Even though I had seen the life go out of him, I still could not believe that he was dead. Maybe it was all a mistake. Maybe he was still alive. Maybe if I just knelt in the same place long enough, maybe if I prayed hard enough, he would come back to me.

It was crazy thinking and I knew it but that did not stop these thoughts from swirling around in my head.

"You must go now," Béla said so softly that it was almost a whisper. "Take Heidi and go back to the Feketes. It's the only place where you are safe."

I knew Béla was right but I could not bring myself to take even one step away from my father. "I can't leave him lying here in the gutter," I said softly.

"I will take care of everything," Béla promised. "Please leave it to me. Take the car and go."

"My father deserves a proper burial," I said, still hesitating.

Béla nodded. "Of course he does and he will get one."

I hugged my mother and my sister Rose and took Heidi's hand. We made our way to the car and back to the Fekete house. I do not remember what I said to Janika when we returned or how Heidi and I got through the night. Thank God we had each other. I know we cried and held each other until dawn broke over the city. I know it was one of the worst nights of my entire life.

We buried my father the following night in a secret ceremony at the Csorsz cemetery. I don't know how Béla managed the arrangements but I am quite certain he had to pay a substantial bribe to some official to make it happen.

Béla was there of course, as were my mother and Rose. Heidi had to stay with Jozsef, who insisted she work late with him. Rabbi Zucker performed the service and we each placed a handful of dirt over my father's grave. We prayed for his soul and his eternal peace. As is our tradition, Mama and Rose tore the sleeves of their blouses; this is part of the Jewish ceremony that symbolizes the rendering of our hearts at the loss of a loved one. I knew that I could not walk around with a torn sleeve without someone suspecting I was Jewish so, instead, I tore the inside seam of my dress, keeping my sorrow hidden from the world in the same way I kept so much about myself hidden.

By any standard, it wasn't much of a service but, in those days, it was an extraordinary event and much more than a Jewish family could expect. Even this truncated service brought great comfort to all of us. I was sure that my father would have been proud.

You really cannot imagine how comforting traditional ceremonies like funerals can be until they are taken away from you.

Still, I was overwhelmed by my father's death. Nothing had prepared me for life without him. My father was my rock and the one person I knew would always protect and care for me, no matter what. Now I felt like a tightrope walker who was suddenly working without a safety net.

Yes, Papa's death left a huge hole in my heart and, even though I would survive to name one of my sons after him, that hole has never been completely repaired. My father was a good man, an honorable man and a humble, faithful servant to God. He did not deserve such a painful, murderous death and there is a part of me that still cannot forgive a God that allowed Papa to die that way.

Those feelings I had when my father died—of desperation, grief and loneliness—have never entirely left me. I still grieve for my dear Papa and pray for his soul almost every day.

There are some deaths from which we never recover and, though death was all around me on those last days before liberation, the death of my father was the one from which I have yet to recover.

Chapter Seventeen

B éla drove us all home from the cemetery. We dropped my
   mother and sister Rose off at the Swiss safe house where
they were still living and the Rabbi got out of the car a few
blocks later.

We were driving over the Erzsebet Bridge when I asked Béla
to pull over and park on the other side of the Danube. "I need
some air," I told him.

Béla stopped, turned off the ignition and sat staring out
the window. In the distance, across the river, we could see the
lights sparkling on the opposite shore. If I closed my eyes, I
could pretend that this was just an ordinary night in Budapest
and I was just a single woman alone with a handsome man
on a summer evening. But, of course, as hard as I tried, I could
not erase the events of the past few days and the turmoil that
I was feeling.

Béla and I both opened our doors at the same moment and
got out of the car. We walked to the abutment overlooking a
familiar walking path. I remembered when Imre and I had
strolled along the riverbank, on this very path, sometime last

summer. How very long ago and far away that seemed right now. Did I really have a life before the war? Was there actually a time when my only concern was finding a pretty dress to wear and coaxing some young man into taking me for a summer's walk? What had happened to that girl?

I sighed and shoved my hands deeper into my pockets.

"It is still so beautiful here," Béla remarked, as if he were reading my thoughts.

"Yes," I agreed. "Budapest will always be a lovely city."

"I used to come here all the time to gaze at the lights." Béla stopped for a moment to gaze up at the sky.

"Those days are long gone," I remarked, perhaps a bit more sharply than I intended.

Béla started to reply but turned his head at the sound of someone shouting orders. He glanced at me with an alarmed expression on his face, then raised his finger to his lips to stop our conversation.

We looked down below to the walking path to see an armed gang of Arrow Cross militia brutally pushing several dozen Jews towards the river. The bright yellow Stars of David on their clothing seemed to glow in the soft moonlight. The guards were barking orders for the people to move faster, to pick up the pace, to get going or else they'd end up in the river.

I craned my neck to get a closer view of whatever was taking place on the riverbank. "What's going on?" I whispered to Béla. A sudden chill ran up my spine and I shivered in the night air.

But he put his hand lightly over my mouth to silence me and gently pushed me deeper into the shadows of a tall tree. I could see fear in his eyes. I became alarmed because I'd never known him to be afraid before.

Then we heard the militia ordering the prisoners to remove their coats and shoes and put them into designated piles.

When the prisoners failed to act quickly, the guards screamed even louder.

I was trying to figure out what the Arrow Cross wanted with the coats and shoes and was completely unprepared for what happened next.

The men, women and, yes, children were lined up along the riverbank. They were shivering from the cold and the rain and most of them had crossed their arms over their chests and stomped their feet to keep warm. Some of them were clutching hold of each other. The children seemed to think it was some kind of game although some of them were crying for their mothers or fathers. One of the militia fired a shot into the air and ordered everyone to be silent. A hush fell over the group. One elderly woman sank to her knees and vomited on the grass.

The Arrow Cross guards stood in front of the line of people. They waited for a long tense moment and then, almost in unison, each one of the guards raised up his rifle, as if on cue. Another moment passed. None of the prisoners tried to run or even protest. I don't think they realized what was coming next. I certainly didn't, even though it was obvious, I suppose.

There was an explosion of sound, like a giant clap of thunder on a summer evening, and a blast of fire seemed to shoot out of the weapons.

All of the prisoners—young and old alike—went down in an explosion of body parts and blood spurts. The impact of the bullets caused some of the people to twirl around as if they were dancers, while others seemed to be pulled backwards by an invisible rope. A small child of no more than three or four sailed through the air like a rag doll and dropped into the rough water. The elderly woman collapsed into a heap.

Every last one of them fell—too startled to even cry out

or protest. Most tumbled down into the Danube. Others, the ones still on the riverbank, were shoved and kicked into the water by the soldiers.

Some of the bodies sank immediately. Others floated before they disappeared beneath the surface of the water. A few seemed to expand—almost gently—then drift off towards the other side of the river.

The guards began sorting through the coats and shoes, picking out the ones they wanted and tossing the rejects into the water.

Although it happened right before my eyes, I could not believe it was 'real.' It was like watching the worst conceivable nightmare projected in front of you but you know it is not a nightmare, that it is actually happening. I remembered once seeing a painting by Hieronymous Bosch and being horrified by the images of death and destruction. Now they were here, undeniable, confronting me; death and destruction were painted in the blood of real life on the banks of my beloved Danube.

The sight of those bodies falling into the river was like seeing civilization unspool before my eyes. My brain was breaking up into a million shattered pieces. I could almost feel my soul leaving my body. I thought perhaps I had died in that round of gunfire and this was my introduction into hell. And, if I weren't dead, would I actually want to go on living here, where such an event could happen?

I was anchored to that abutment as if I were made of concrete. I might have stayed glued there if Béla had not pulled me back to reality. He grabbed my hand and pulled me from the path. With great urgency he dragged me towards the car. My legs were jelly; it took all my determination to keep moving them.

We got back into the car and, tires squealing, sped away from the unbelievable, unforgettable scene at the Danube.

Shocked silence filled the car.

"The world has gone completely mad. We must tell someone what we have witnessed!" I said to Béla with great urgency.

He shrugged as he maneuvered the car into a stream of traffic. "There's no one to tell," he said in such a matter-of-fact manner that I thought I heard him incorrectly or, more accurately, that he did not hear me correctly.

"The police...no of course not; the Arrow Cross *are* the police. But there must be someone! *Anyone!* Béla, we cannot allow these criminals to continue to slaughter my people!" I shouted as if he did not understand what was happening. I began pounding my fist on the dashboard.

But of course he understood. In fact, he understood a lot more than I did. "There are people who are trying their best to help," he said calmly, the way one would talk to a child who was having a temper tantrum. "We must hang on until the Soviets break through and defeat the Germans."

"So then we trade one monster for another."

"What do you suggest we do, Gizi?" It was the first time he had ever snapped at me and, all of a sudden I realized he was just as frustrated and angry as I.

I stared out the window of the car. The familiar landmarks of the city passed by. Here was a café where I once danced with my father. And here was a shop where my mother bought fabrics. How could the world look so normal when everything around us was sheer insanity?

I took a deep breath. "Before my father died he told me not to believe in miracles," I said. "He believed that God would take care of us and look what happened to him. He told me to do what needed to be done and that is what I am going to do from now on. Will you help me?"

"I promised your father I would not involve you in anything dangerous," Béla said, shaking his head.

"My father released us from that vow when he died. Béla, you told me my father didn't want me to get involved with your 'friends' but my father is no longer here and we are far beyond promises made to protect little girls. I am on my own now and I want to be part of the fight. I know there is something that I can be doing. I need this Béla, I really do. I don't think I can stay sane if I can't do something to help."

Béla swerved the car to the side of the road and turned off the engine. He turned to me. "Are you sure about this, Gizi? Really sure? You and Heidi are relatively safe now and can probably wait out this war, maybe even in Switzerland."

"No, Béla. No more waiting. Right or wrong, Emil chose his destiny and so must I. If we're all going to die in this war—and it looks like we are—then I'd rather be doing something meaningful with whatever time I have left. I *have* to make a difference. I have to. For Emil, for my father, but mostly for me. No, being silent, obedient Maria is no longer a possibility for me."

In my heart I knew that the war had come too close and I was ready and willing to fight back in whatever way I could. I would not be taken to the banks of the Danube and tossed into the river like so much garbage. I would not be marched into a gas chamber. That would not be my fate. I would help those I could help. I would go down kicking and screaming and fighting to the last breath.

But I could see that Béla was still not convinced. He opened his mouth to protest and I put my hand over his lips and shook my head.

"And don't tell me that it's too dangerous...tell it to those innocent children who are now floating in the river!"

Béla sighed and slowly nodded. He started the car and eased back into traffic.

"Where are we going?" I asked.

Béla shrugged. "To meet my friends, of course," he said.

Chapter Eighteen

Winter swept into Budapest with a vengeance that year. It got cold very early and by mid-October there were hailstorms and sleet. By December, the streets were covered with dirty gray snow and great slabs of ice made it difficult to navigate the sidewalks. There was a shortage of coal so we froze at night and burned whatever we could find during the day. Janika's influential father managed to supply the house with some wood and coal but even for those in such exalted positions, anything that generated heat was a rare commodity.

During those months after my father died, I lived a complicated double life. By day I was Maria, the good Catholic girl and obedient house servant who left the Fekete house only for Sunday mass, weekly church services and church-related volunteer duties. With Janika's approval I became more and more active in my church and was called out frequently to help with various church businesses, or at least that is what I told her. She commented that I was becoming more devout than ever but how could she complain about that? As a good Christian woman (which is how Janika described herself), she had to believe my lies. Away from the spying eyes of Janika Fekete, I was Gizi, the Jewish patriot who helped with whatever task was assigned to me by an elaborate underground network of resistance fighters.

I lived with the Feketes for my survival but I worked with the underground for my sanity.

I often took care of baby Gusztav while Janika spent time with her friends. They all continued to pretend life was normal despite the war, which seemed merely an inconvenience to their hair appointments, ladies luncheons and card games. Gusztav was now almost four months old. He was a strapping, healthy baby, big for his age and always cheerful. His smiling face and bright eyes were the only joyous notes in that gloomy house. Despite the terror of our situation, the sight of a happy baby never failed to lift my spirits. Holding Gusztav always reminded me that we were fighting for future generations as well as our own survival.

But Gusztav was only a tiny light in a very dark season. Amid the death and destruction all around us, Heidi and I worked hard to keep up our spirits. We tried to remain hopeful as the Allied forces advanced on the Nazi front. For most of us, it was obvious that it was only a matter of time before Hitler's regime toppled and his reign of terror ended. However, that end could not come soon enough, especially for the Jews in Budapest.

As soon as the Hungarian government was turned over to that murdering bastard, Ferenc Szálazi, the stateless Jews around the city escaped as quickly as possible, warning those who remained that we were in terrible danger. The Hungarian Jews, who had been protected for so long, did not respond and those who remained were in constant danger. In addition to the German deportations, the Arrow Cross went on a murderous rampage, determined to kill as many Jews as possible before the war ended. It was mass slaughter on a scale never before seen in the "civilized" world.

As for my family, we were among those who mistakenly thought we were still relatively safe in our own country. Most of us continued to hold tight and pray for salvation from the evil forces let loose around us. My mother and sister Rose were back in the Swiss safe house with their official documentation and visas from the Swiss government. We were all hoping to find a way out of Hungary but, even with our official visas, it was difficult to arrange transportation, which had become exorbitantly expensive.

Heidi and I remained with the Feketes, keeping up the pretense of our fake personas. Although Jozsef had long known the secret of our real identities, he remained entirely captivated by Heidi and therefore had a stake in making sure Janika never found out about us, or I should say, about Heidi and himself.

One cold winter afternoon during a fierce snowstorm that had closed all the bridges around the city to traffic, I was folding baby clothes while Gusztav slept peacefully in his little crib. The phone rang and I hurried to answer it.

It was Leo, a friend I had met through Béla. He must have had an urgent message or he would never have called me at the Feketes. When I assured him that it was indeed me on the phone (using a secret password we had for just that reason), Leo said, "The gate at Magdolna Street. The church on Kállay." He hung up without another word. I knew what I needed to do.

I went to the hall closet to get my coat.

Janika called down from upstairs. "Maria, make sure the baby is covered; this chill will make him sick."

"Yes, Mrs. Fekete, I know," I said, walking over to the crib to check that the swaddling was tightly wrapped around him. I could see that Guzstav was dreaming, his eyelids fluttered and he gave out a squeaky cry.

"Hush, hush, little boy," I cooed. "Everything will be all right." I patted his tummy till he settled down and his face relaxed.

I could hear Janika coming down the stairs. "Who was that on the phone?" she called from the top of the stairs.

"Just a wrong number," I replied.

Janika walked into the parlor wearing a heavy woolen robe. "Why are you in your coat?" she asked. "Where are you going in the middle of this storm?"

I withdrew a wool scarf from my pocket and wrapped it around my head. "Mass, of course. It's Sunday," I said with a shrug.

Janika shook her head. "Even in this weather? Oh, you are so devoted to the church, Maria; you put us all to shame. I almost forgot that it is Sunday. My days are so mixed up because of this child," she placed a hand on the baby's head and patted him gently. Despite her many flaws, Janika was very kind and sweet to her baby. I often wondered how she could be so loving to her own child and so hateful to anyone else's. "If you are going to mass, would you be a dear, Maria, and light a Novena candle for our brave Arrow Cross men? They've been called to hold the eastern edge."

Janika called herself a good Christian woman but I'd yet to see her attend any church. She smiled at me as if we were the closest friends. Then she lifted Gusztav from the crib and cradled him in her arms.

I was glad to hear that the Arrow Cross was being summoned away. The fewer of them on our streets, the better it would be.

"Of course Mrs. Fekete," I replied. "I'll surely say a prayer for those who need it most."

I turned quickly, before anything else escaped from my lips, and hurried out of the house.

It took me about an hour to reach the gate on Magdolna Street. It had snowed all night and it was difficult to walk through the many drifts that had accumulated. But the blanket of snow cast a calm and peaceful demeanor to the city and I was grateful for the silence, no matter how temporary it was.

I stood in a doorway near the gate for about twenty minutes. Then a woman wearing the yellow Star of David on her coat appeared. Three small children, wrapped in rags against the winter weather, were holding hands as the woman lead them toward me. They were small enough to fit through a crack in the gate. The woman, who I did not recognized, kissed each child at the fence. The children were so bundled up in rags that I could not tell if they were boys or girls.

The woman's cheeks were stained with tears that I thought might freeze on her skin. "Take good care of my children," she whispered to me in a voice that was frightened, tender and hopeful at the same time.

"I will," I promised and reached out to squeeze the woman's arm. This was a scene that I had witnessed numerous times in the past four months but it never felt any less traumatic. How terrible it must feel for a mother to have to give over her children to total strangers. What an awful choice to make: abandonment or possible slaughter. I could only imagine this poor mother's pain.

I gathered the children together and told them to hold onto each other's hands. They silently obeyed me. We walked away from the gate. None of the children turned around for a last glance at their mother.

In a few minutes we arrived at the church at Kállay Street, only a few blocks from the ghetto. I ushered the children into a pew near the confessionals in the back of the church. Though there wasn't much heat inside, it was still warmer than the street. The children looked at me and I was taken by the quiet resignation in their faces.

My best guess was that they were nine, seven and six years old. The older two were girls and the youngest was a dark-haired boy with deep brown eyes. They were all painfully thin.

I told the older girl to go into the far left confessional. She looked sternly at her two younger siblings. "Dora, Jonah, you do whatever this lady tells you. You understand?" She smoothed down her hair and straightened her shoulders as she made her way to the confessional. She was heartbreakingly mature. The two younger children followed her with their eyes, then looked up at me.

I waited until the girl had been gone for a few minutes, then directed Jonah to follow his sister to the same place. He nodded at me and walked away. Dora went a few minutes later.

All three children went into the confessional but none of them came out.

I didn't know what would happen to these children once I had led them into the confessional. In the underground, we were told only what we needed to know in order to perform our part of the procedure. I prayed that the children would make it out of Hungary, out of Europe, to someplace safe. I prayed that one day they would be reunited with their mother. Of course, it was not my habit to pray in church but I thought it could not hurt their chances if I offered prayers to whatever God would listen.

I often think about those children and all the others we tried so hard to rescue. I wonder what happened to them.

Two days later, Béla and I carried sacks of food to the same ghetto on Magdolna Street where I had picked up the three children. Béla had a source that supplied the underground with black market groceries that had been sent to Hungary from somewhere in Germany. Getting the food into the ghetto was another problem.

A hole had been cut in the fence covering the back alley of the ghetto, a place not regularly patrolled by the Arrow Cross. The space was hidden behind a big shrub and was just big enough for me to slip through (especially since I had lost so much weight in the past six months.) Once I was safely inside, Béla handed the sacks of food to me. I carried these into the ghetto and delivered them to the Rabbi for whoever needed them the most. Usually we were able to pass along enough food for several families. It was never a lot—it was never enough—but it was something. Every last crust of bread counted.

It was dark by the time we finished our delivery that evening. Though it was probably foolish, we decided to walk back to the Fekete house, enjoying the chill in the air and the beautiful clear sky.

I told Béla how I had managed to take a group over to pick up some broken furniture. We were bringing the furniture to the ghetto so to burn for fuel. Daniel, our usual driver, had a broken arm and I had only a few minutes to figure out that kind of stick shift, which was different than other vehicles I drove. Béla was laughing about how many times I stalled out the engine before managing to find first gear.

We were standing on the front steps to the Fekete house

when I reminded Béla to hush his laughing. "You'll wake the sleeping dragon," I warned.

"Too late," he said with a grin, pointing at the front door as it slowly opened.

Janika stood in the doorway with a surprised look on her face. Her hair was wrapped in a scarf and her face still bore traces of white cold cream. She was wearing a floor length nightgown, covered by Jozsef's winter coat. Her feet were bare. "Oh! It's only you," she exclaimed, sounding relieved. "I heard noises and didn't know what to think."

"Yes, it's just us, Mrs. Fekete," Béla offered, with a smile that never failed to charm my employer.

Janika wrapped the wool coat more tightly around her and shivered in the night air. "Well, you never know these days who might be lurking about the street." She glanced to the right and to the left. "We can't be too careful. If it's not the Jews, then it's the communists. Lately, it just seems we are not safe in our own homes." She sniffed the air. "Isn't that right, Mr. Stollár?"

Before he could answer, I extended my hand to Béla in a kind of formal gesture. I wanted to save him from having to answer Janika. "Well, then. Good night Béla," I said.

"Good night, Maria," he replied with the same bemused formality and squeezed my hand lightly.

I nodded at Janika and walked past her into the house. I stood in the hallway to remove my coat.

"She's really a lovely girl," I heard Janika say to Béla in a loud whisper. "But her sympathy to the Jews? Well, I guess I understand, she's from common country stock and doesn't realize how much those Jew bastards have taken from us. Isn't that right, Mr. Stollár?"

"Yes," I heard Béla say, "That's right, Mrs. Fekete, Maria *is* a lovely girl."

He said good night and tipped his hat, I am quite sure. Then I heard his footsteps echoing down the concrete steps.

Chapter Nineteen

⁓❦⁓

A week later, I got another call from Leo, telling me to be down at a specific pier on the Danube. But Janika was playing bridge at Mrs. Perepatits's house and I was watching the baby. I chewed my lip, wondering what to do.

If I was needed at the pier, it probably meant that a shipment of either food or medical supplies was coming. And, if they had called me on a weekday, then it probably meant no one else was available for the assignment. (I usually got called to work on Sundays, when I could use church as an excuse to leave the house.) This must be an emergency, so I had to figure out a way to get to that pier. But what about the baby? I could not take him with me and I certainly could not leave him alone in the house. I paced the hallway trying to come up with a viable plan.

After a few minutes, I raced upstairs and dressed Gusztav in his warmest snowsuit. Then I swaddled him in two blankets and gently placed him in his carriage. He was still so sleepy that he did not protest.

I quickly changed into woolen pants and a heavy sweater

and put on my warmest coat and hat. I borrowed the woolen gloves that my sister had just finished knitting the night before. These gloves were meant for one of the families in the ghetto but I did not think Heidi would mind if I borrowed them for this one assignment.

Locking the front door behind me, I hurried down the street, pushing Gusztav in his carriage. He seemed happy to be going on an adventure with me.

I walked to Jozsef's office. I left the baby carriage on the street and picked up Gusztav. The little angel did not even awaken; he just nuzzled his head on my shoulder.

My plan was to leave the baby with Heidi for the few hours I would need at the pier. In the best of all possible scenarios, Jozsef would be out of the office and I could return for the baby without him or Janika ever knowing.

Well, that did not happen. I left the carriage on the street and let myself into the office, being very quiet so as to not wake the baby. I was surprised to see that Heidi was not at her desk in the outer office. Then I heard the sound of a conversation coming from Jozsef's inner office. I recognized the voices: Heidi and Jozsef were speaking.

I turned towards Jozsef's private office. The door was slightly ajar and I could hear Joszef talking to Heidi. Should I knock or should I wait until Heidi came back out? I looked at my watch. If I waited much longer I would be late meeting my contact at the pier. I raised my hand to knock on the door but the sound of their voices made me hesitate.

"You're not listening to me," Jozsef said in a loud and somewhat threatening tone of voice. "I've got to leave the city soon. Soviet tanks are ransacking the hills just east of us. They'll be here before you know it. Those Red bastards rape and rob innocent Christians. They're heartless pricks, absolutely heartless."

"Oh, so now *you're* afraid?" Heidi asked and I winced hearing the blatant scorn in her voice.

"In a few days, the Reds will have surrounded Budapest, it's inevitable," Joszef sniffed, not really answering her question. "I do not wish to deal with them, that is all. But you are not to worry." I heard the sound of papers shuffling, as if he was rifling through a file cabinet or his desk drawer. "When I go, of course, I will take you with me."

That is when my hand froze in mid-air. I could not believe what he had just suggested to Heidi.

Heidi barked out a laugh. "And what of Janika and your beloved son?" she asked with a somewhat amused tone to her voice. This surprised me. Was she actually taking him seriously?

Jozsef made a clicking sound with his tongue. "Have you forgotten that my wife is the daughter of one of Hungary's most influential politicians? Papa Rigo will see to Janika and his grandson. That old blowhard never liked me anyway. My family will be just fine without me."

I glanced at the sleeping baby in my arms and wondered how any father could even consider abandoning such a gift from heaven. I held Gusztav more tightly to reassure him that he was loved.

Then I heard a loud smashing noise as something—perhaps a coffee cup—was thrown across the room and crashed on the wall or floor. "You coward!" Heidi screamed. "You'd leave your wife and your baby behind to face the Soviets while you run away like a dog with your Jewish mistress! What kind of a man are you?"

"You wish to stay here then?" Joszef indignantly replied. "You'd rather trust your fate to those filthy scoundrels than take your chances with me? The Reds have no love for you Jews. They'll finish off Hitler's work with pleasure. You'd be better off with me, I can assure you of that."

I heard the sound of a hand slapping against flesh and I could only assume that Heidi had finally struck back.

She came storming out of the office, slamming the door behind her. She looked at me without registering any surprise that I was standing there in the office holding the baby in my arms. In my sister's eyes I could see a look of triumph and, after all those months of she had felt like a victim, it made me proud of her.

"Go then!" Jozsef shouted from his office. "You're nothing but a cheap whore and you know it! Maybe I'll turn you in to the Arrow Cross before I leave this godforsaken country!"

Heidi waved a hand at him, no longer intimidated by his empty threats. We had discussed this a million times; Joszef could not report us without revealing his own participation in our disguise. Harboring a Jew was almost as great a crime as being a Jew.

Heidi slipped into her coat, took my arm, and led me out of the office.

On the street, I explained that I needed to leave Gusztav with her for a few hours. She asked where I was going but I told her it was better she did not know. I was sorry we did not have time to talk about what had just happened with Joszef but she waved a hand at me as if to indicate it did not matter. "That lousy bastard is going to abandon his family just when they need him the most. He's a terrible person and I hope he rots in hell for all his sins," she exclaimed passionately. It was wonderful to hear her finally express her anger. For too long, she had been holding it in.

Heidi took the baby from my arms and gently returned him

to the carriage. I kissed her cheek and hurried down the street to catch a bus to the pier.

It took me about forty minutes to reach my destination. Once on the banks of the Danube, I hid in the bushes with Leo and another member of our group whose name I did not know. We waited for more than an hour, until a large motorboat appeared from the distance and docked at the pier.

The man steering the boat signaled us to pull it closer to the pier and he tossed out a line. We quickly unloaded several large crates of medical supplies that, according to their labels, had come all the way from the United Kingdom. We carried these up the hill and into a waiting milk truck. Then we drove to St. Anne's Hospital in the Buda section of the city.

St. Anne's was a legitimate Catholic hospital but everyone knew it was the only medical facility in Budapest where Jews were not turned away.

The streets were difficult to navigate as gangs of Arrow Cross soldiers were patrolling. We avoided them as best we could and finally made it to the hospital, where the crates were unloaded under the supervision of a harried young doctor.

I had been planning to leave at that point—if I hurried I could make it back to the Fekete house in time to prepare a quick dinner. But the doctor asked if I could possibly stay to help feed the patients. Apparently, neither the nurse on duty nor the woman who cooked for the hospital had shown up that morning and they had no one else who could help. The hospital was overcrowded with patients, especially a group of children who had been injured when their orphanage had collapsed in an air strike two days earlier.

How could I possibly say no?

I thought about Janika for about a minute and decided that, after Heidi's argument with Jozsef, our time at the Fekete house was probably limited to another day—two at the very most—and here was something I could do to really help.

I spent the next few hours comforting the children as well as I could. Several had broken limbs, which the doctor had tried to set into makeshift casts. Others were badly cut and had been stitched up and bandaged. The doctor was tending to two youngsters who had been burned. All of the children were hungry. And though there was nothing I could do medically for them, I could get them something to eat. There was not much food in the hospital kitchen. I could find only a sack of potatoes that someone had left on the counter and a bit of milk. I made mashed potatoes and fed as many children as I could from that pot.

I was with a little boy with a bandage wrapped around his head when I heard a loud commotion from the street outside the hospital. I went to the window and was startled to see a large contingent of Arrow Cross soldiers marching towards the hospital. They had guns and clubs in their hands and were shouting all kinds of nasty, anti-Semitic slurs.

The sight of one Arrow Cross soldier was enough to frighten me but seeing an angry mob of lawless, probably drunk, murderous thugs all in one place was really a terrifying sight.

What would they do to all these defenseless children?

There was only one person I could call at the moment and that was Béla.

He answered the phone on the first ring and told me to gather the children and take them to the safest place I could find in the hospital. He would get there as quickly as possible and he'd bring help.

I led the children down to the basement of the hospital. They did not protest or even seem surprised when I instructed them to move quickly on the stairs. I settled them in the damp and musty cellar as well as I could, covering them with spare blankets. Then I sat with them and prayed.

I knew that Béla and his "friends" had collected a makeshift arsenal of weapons and, if ever they were needed, it was today. I had not locked the front doors to the hospital before I'd come downstairs. The lock wouldn't keep the Arrow Cross out of the hospital, but it might at least delay them for a bit.

I raced up the stairs and down the hallway to the front of the hospital. I turned the locks on the heavy doors and tested them to make sure they were securely locked.

Outside I could see the Arrow Cross soldiers coming towards us from across the park on the other side of the street. From the left came Béla and a group of ragtag partisans, who rushed forward to block the entrance to the hospital. Béla led the charge.

The Arrow Cross soldiers—who outnumbered the partisans by at least four to one—were screaming for them to leave.

"Go away!" they yelled. "We are just after the Jews. It's our right to kill the scum before the Reds get here!"

Béla and his men tried to reason with the angry mob, begging them to leave the patients alone.

"There are only innocent people here!"

"They are sick and injured."

"Go back to your Nazi masters."

The screaming continued for several long minutes and I knew this would not end well.

Suddenly a shot rang out and both groups of fighters scrambled for cover. Some ran towards the hospital, others in the opposite direction. The soldiers were far more disorganized than Béla's partisans, who at least stayed together in one group on the hospital steps.

Then all hell broke loose.

Gunfire was exchanged from both sides of the building.

I ran to the marble column in the lobby and hid behind it.

More guns were fired; men were still screaming. The glass on the entrance doors shattered into a thousand pieces. Shards of glass skittered across the floor of the lobby.

From behind the column I could see Béla and about a dozen partisans. Smoke from the gunfire obscured my view but it was clear that the partisans were holding off the soldiers. Béla was shouting orders as one of his men took a bullet in the leg and went down. "Fall back into the hospital," I heard Béla scream. "We'll make our stand there!"

The partisans continued firing their pistols as they backed into the lobby.

"Béla, we need more ammunition," one of the fighters screamed.

"It's almost gone," Béla yelled back. "Find cover."

I stuck my head out from behind the column and Béla spotted me at once. I signaled for him to come to the column and he started towards me. That's when a bullet pierced his upper chest, flinging him to the floor.

I didn't stop to think. I ran out and scrambled along the marble floor until I reached him. I grabbed the collar of his coat and dragged him across the lobby to the column, leaving a trail of blood on the marble.

Béla pulled himself into a sitting position and slumped against the column.

"Don't you dare die on me!" I screamed at him over the roar of the gunfire. I tried to pull back his jacket to inspect his wound but he waved away my hand.

"No one is going to die," he said, but blood dripped down from the side of his mouth and I knew he was wrong.

With his free hand, Béla took a pistol from his waistband and gave it to me.

I shook my head and waved away the gun. "No, no, no! I can't kill anyone," I exclaimed, shocked that he thought I could. I tried to wipe the blood from his lips but he pushed my hand aside.

"Who killed Emil? Who killed Imre? Who killed your father?" Béla asked in a hoarse voice.

Tears were streaming down my face and I felt like I was choking on the thick air. What did he want from me? "Béla, please," I said, "I don't understand. This is madness."

"Who killed your father? Who killed all those children? Who shot those innocent people and threw them in the river? Say it, Gizi, say it!"

Anger flared up from deep inside me. "The Nazis! They killed them, you son of a bitch!" I spit out in a sudden rage.

Béla slumped over on the floor and I knew he was dying. "Yes," he said, "the Nazis, not you. None of this is your fault, my darling Gizi."

He reached up a bloody hand and touched my cheek. There was so much I wanted to tell him, so many things I needed to thank him for but hadn't got the chance.

A moment later, Béla's eyes went blank and he died.

I barely had time to react.

At that same moment, I looked up to see that the Arrow Cross soldiers had broken through the doors and were in hand-to-hand combat with the remaining partisans.

One of the soldiers ran towards me. He was huge and he was fast. His face was contorted with rage.

I screamed as I raised Béla's pistol. I held the gun with both hands and closed my eyes. I pulled the trigger. I opened my eyes and saw that man go down, blood exploding from his skull.

I did not wait to see if he was breathing. I turned and ran down the hallway until I found the basement stairs.

I had actually killed another human being and I was not the least bit sorry.

I yanked open the door and locked it behind me.

Chapter Twenty

I thought we would never get out of that basement alive.
The Arrow Cross soldiers were all over the hospital, ransacking the place and killing whoever they could find. We heard the sounds of women screaming, glass shattering, furniture being overturned and other random violence. I could only imagine what was going on upstairs.

So far the soldiers had not yet discovered the basement.

I put the children in a tight circle and we held hands in that dark, cold cellar. I was prepared to die and I was steeling myself to witness the massacre of all these innocent children (as if I could possibly prepare for that!). I prayed for strength and courage. I prayed for Béla and for my father to watch over and help me be brave in front of the children.

Suddenly we felt a massive rumbling, as if the entire building was being shaken. It felt like the wrath of God was bearing down upon us. (Later we discovered that that was the sound made by Soviet tanks on Budapest's cobblestone streets.)

A few minutes later, a cannon thundered into the building, rocking the very walls and foundation. In the basement, it felt like an earthquake. The floor beneath us rose up, then slammed down. Cement dust from the walls flaked off like winter snow, filling the air with an acrid odor and making it difficult to breath. The children started screaming and we did not try to silence them. Amidst all the noise and confusion, their thin voices could hardly be heard. And it was clear that the Arrow Cross had more important considerations.

So did we.

"We've got to get out of this cellar," the doctor said to me. "The whole building could collapse on us."

I nodded and we told the children to stand up and follow us.

There was a window on the other end of the cellar but it was jammed shut. The doctor took a broken steel chair and smashed it against the glass. The window shattered. He quickly removed the leftover glass and climbed through the hole.

I stayed inside and boosted the children, one by one, through the window and onto the street where they all escaped in different directions.

Outside, it was total mayhem.

Three Soviet tanks were positioned in front of the hospital, their turrets turning in all directions. Cannons were being fired at the hospital and the nearby buildings, creating massive piles of rubble. From inside the hospital, Arrow Cross militia and Nazi soldiers were firing at the tanks.

Then, from the streets, a large group of Red Army infantry, fully armed and firing their weapons approached.

The Arrow Cross gang suddenly burst outside into the daylight with their firearms blazing.

A machine gun mounted on one of the tanks delivered a staccato burst of lead right into the group; several members of the militia were ripped to shreds as body parts sprayed across the hospital steps. The battle for the hospital was over in only a few minutes, as the Red infantry totally outnumbered the ragtag Arrow Cross contingency. As soon as it was apparent that no enemy was left to fight at the hospital, the tanks turned to move deeper in to the city. The gunfire became more and more faint and the smoke and smell of cordite started to evaporate.

The doctor looked at me, grabbed my shoulders and held me in a tight hug. He kissed me on the mouth, then disappeared back into the hospital. I didn't even know his name.

I looked up at the bodies on the steps. I took a deep breath and forced myself not to think about Béla. There would be plenty of time for that later.

As I made my way back to the Feketes' house, people came out of their houses and gathered in small groups. No one was talking. Men and women roamed the city in a kind of daze, looking up and down the streets—looking, I think, for someone to tell them who was in charge. All Budapest seemed shrouded in a stunned silence.

What had just happened?

The streets were covered with the broken and bleeding bodies of Arrow Cross militia and Nazi soldiers. They were everywhere and it suddenly occurred to us that we were liberated. The war was ending.

As if on some kind of silent signal, the people in the streets began to cheer and joyous laughter rang out. There was dancing in the streets.

It was over; it was finally over!

With all the chaos and crowds, it took me several hours to

make it back to the Fekete house. As I walked up the steps to the brownstone, I realized that I was covered in dirt and in Béla's blood.

I opened the front door and there was Janika. She was holding Gusztav in one hand and throwing clothes into a trunk with her free hand. Her hair was disheveled and she was sweating through her cotton dress.

"Maria! Hurry! We've got to pack," she exclaimed. "The radio said the Red Army was at the city gates and it just went dead! We've got to get out of here. I don't know where to find Jozsef; he doesn't answer his phone. We don't know what's happening!"

I stood in the doorway and watched her for a moment. Where did she think she was going with that big trunk?

"The Reds have liberated the city," I said, with a smile on my face. It thrilled me to be the one delivering this information to Janika Fekete.

"That's impossible you idiot!" she screeched, waving her arm and knocking a white vase off the table in the hallway. The vase shattered on the floor and Janika cried out. "Now look what you made me do!" she wailed, as if the broken vase was her biggest concern at the moment.

"I'm sorry, Mrs. Fekete, but the war is over and you lost," I said, enjoying her agitation. "The tanks are on the streets; the infantry has landed. I've seen them with my own eyes. It's safe now."

"Safe!" she exclaimed. "Are you crazy? The Reds will persecute us instead of those filthy Jews. We've got to get out of the city!"

"Yes, well that's your problem now," I said with satisfaction. "I've only come back to collect my sister."

"Sister?" Janika asked, her forehead wrinkling with confusion. "Who is your sister?"

"Eva Vargas and Maria Kovach are not sisters. But Heidi and Gizella Kornfeld have always been the closest sisters," I told her with pride.

Janika's jaw dropped down to her chest and the surprise on her face was almost comical. She was too stunned to speak and could only sputter out a few syllables.

"But...but...how?"

"Mrs. Fekete I want to thank you for the *mitzvah* you provided by giving us room and board this past year. Without your help, my sister and I never would have survived."

"You...are...JEWS??" she hissed, still not believing what I was saying to her.

I nodded my head.

Janika stepped closer to me and slapped my cheek with the palm of her hand.

She hit me hard but I barely felt the sting. I smiled at her. Then I touched Gusztav's cheek. "I forgive you," I said to the baby.

I looked up the stairs and saw Heidi standing there with a suitcase in her hand. She was smiling at me.

She came dancing down and kissed my cheek—the same cheek Janika had just slapped.

Heidi turned to Janika. "*Shalom aleikhem,*" she said to her, "which means good-bye and peace be with you."

Heidi threaded her arm through mine and together we walked out of the Fekete house for the very last time.

Heidi had one more stop in mind before we went to find Mama and Rose.

She paused to talk to a group of Russian soldiers, then lead them to Joszef's office.

As we walked up the street, we saw Jozsef tossing boxes into the trunk of his car. He slammed the lid shut and loaded his briefcase and a suitcase into the back seat.

Heidi pointed to Jozsef. "That's him," she said to the Soviet soldier.

The soldier yelled at Joszef to stop.

Joszef looked up and jumped into his car. But before he could start the engine, soldiers dragged him out into the street.

"This is a mistake," Jozsef screeched. "Please, you must listen to me! I am an innocent citizen! My father-in-law..." One of the soldiers slammed him in the face with the butt of his rifle. Blood spurted out of his mouth, as did two of his front teeth. Jozsef wailed like a baby, begging for mercy but to no avail.

My sister stared at her former employer with a stone cold look in her eye. She smiled as she watched the soldiers slam Joszef into the back of a truck, just across the street from where Andras had been shot to death a few months ago.

Heidi and I spent the night in the apartment where my mother and my sister Rose were living. We used all our combined ration coupons to buy the ingredients for a chocolate cake and a bottle of red wine. Laughing and crying, we were up all night telling stories about my father, Emil, Imre and Béla. It was our very first feeling of being together again as a family in a long, long time.

The next morning, Heidi and I walked arm in arm along the streets of Budapest, no longer pretending to be anyone other than who we really were. It was a gray overcast day but we didn't care about the weather. The streets were crowded with Soviet tanks, armored vehicles and Red infantry forces.

We came to the large square in Varosmajor Park, across from the embassies, and were surprised to discover that a large crowd had gathered. Hundreds of people stood around talking and pointing to the center of the square. A fog had settled over the area, making it difficult to see what was going on.

Curious, we pushed our way through the crowd to learn what was so interesting to all these people. We finally broke into the open courtyard to see a makeshift gallows had been erected. Ropes hung from the huge ancient elm trees in the center of the square and several corpses hung from the ropes.

The faces of the corpses were swollen and grotesque but they were still recognizable.

There was:

Senior Arrow Cross Counsel Gusztav Rigo (Janika's father.)

Arrow Cross leader Ferenc Szálasi.

Hungarian Prime Minister Döme Sztójay.

And the two dangling corpses on the far right were even more familiar to me: Janika and Joszef Fekete.

I gasped when I recognized them but Heidi didn't hesitate for a moment. She strode over to Jozsef's corpse and spit on his dangling feet.

There was no sign of little Gusztav and I prayed he had been spared. The child, I felt, was innocent of the sins of his parents.

We could not stop staring at the hanging bodies. It was a bizarre spectacle of justice and it filled me with sadness and a profound sense of remorse for all that had been lost in the past few years. Would we ever recover our humanity?

But I did not spend a lot of time thinking about such things.

Heidi and I hurried to the Swiss Embassy. We were there to get our real papers, with our real names on them.

On the steps, Heidi pulled out the false papers that had saved our lives so many times in the past year. I took my papers out of my purse and we stared at them.

"They are worthless now," Heidi said as she ripped hers, flinging the pieces into the air. I watched as the shreds floated down the stairs and into the gutter.

"I am keeping mine," I said, neatly folding them and tucking the papers into the pocket of my coat.

"It's better to forget, Gizi," Heidi protested.

"No, not for me," I replied, patting my pocket. "This will help me to always remember those who sacrificed themselves for us."

Heidi shrugged and wrapped her arm around my shoulder. Then my sister and I walked up the steps of the embassy.

Suddenly, the sun broke through from behind the clouds and, from somewhere in the distance, I heard the unmistakable sounds of Gypsy violins playing once again in Budapest.

EPILOGUE

By David Rich

With the Soviet liberation of Budapest, the so-called 'Hungarian Holocaust' finally ended.

My mother and my Aunt Heidi were not the only Jews to have survived this particular reign of terror by posing as Gentiles. It is estimated that more than 25,000 Jews survived the war in Hungary that way. In Budapest, there was a huge underground network established by resistance fighters to create false papers for these and many other Jews.

These courageous fighters endured and eventually thrived while their tormentors perished and are long gone.

In the late 1940s, my Aunt Heidi moved to Haifa with my grandmother and Aunt Rose. Heidi died in 1984 and, along side my grandmother and my aunt Rose, she was buried in Israel.

Very soon after being liberated, my mother met and married my father, Stephen Rich, a medical doctor who had miraculously survived five years in Dachau. After several years in a displaced persons camp in Germany, my parents and my brother Joe immigrated to New York City in 1949. I was born there a few years later. For most of my childhood, we lived in New City, New York, about a half hour drive from New York City. I moved to Arizona in 1978 and in the 1980, my father retired from his medical practice and my parents moved to Arizona to be closer to me.

After my father died in the mid 1980s, my mother lived a fiercely independent life, full of friends and grandchildren. She never complained, and she never felt sorry for herself for what had happened.

She used to say that Arizona was so hot and dry that she could barely remember the bone chilling cold and sleet of her childhood Hungarian winters and that was fine with her. She never wanted to return to Europe and she was glad that the Arizona sun evaporated her memories and turned them to dust.

My mother outlived all of her contemporaries and she did it with style. Even in the assisted living facility where she spent the last few years of her life, she insisted on getting dressed up every morning. She kept her hair just so, always wore makeup and had her nails done every week. She took great pride in her appearance, her fashionable wardrobe and her trim figure.

My mother died peacefully in her sleep in June 10, 2010, only a few weeks before this book was completed. She was almost 92 years old.

She is buried in Mesa, Arizona but her indomitable spirit lives on in her two surviving sons, four grandchildren and four great grandchildren.

This book was written to honor my mother's remarkable life and to share her courage with the world.

Rest in peace Mother.
We love you, we miss you and we will never forget.

To order an additional copy of *Through Maria's Eyes*
send this form with a check or money order for $13.95
which includes postage and handling to:

DB Rich Productions LLC
872 North Crossbow Court
Chandler AZ 85225

Remember that ½ of all net profits will be donated to
charities as described on the back cover.

If you order 2 or more copies I will include, free of charge,
a DVD of the interview with Gizella(Maria) where she
describes some of her experiences. You can see this at
www.dbrichproductionsllc.com under
Through Maria's Eyes box at the top, just click on it

Name _____

Address _____

_____

_____

Email _____

Amount enclosed _____

Any feedback or comments on this book would be
appreciated and can be sent via email to

d.rich@throughmariaseyes.com